MW00527876

Curly Jack

Curly Jack

McKendree Long

FIVE STAR
A part of Gale, a Cengage Company

Five Star Publishing, a part of Gale, a Cengage Company

LIBRARY OF CONGRESS CATALOGING-IN-PUBLICATION DATA

Names: Long, McKendree R., author.
Title: Curly Jack / McKendree Long.
Description: First Edition. | Waterville, Maine : Five Star, a part of Gale, a Cengage Company, 2021.
Identifiers: LCCN 2019057150 | ISBN 9781432871154 (hardcover)
Subjects: GSAFD: Western stories.
Classification: LCC PS3612.O499 C87 2020 | DDC 813/.6--dc23
LC record available at https://lccn.loc.gov/2019057150

First Edition. First Printing: March 2021
Find us on Facebook—https://www.facebook.com/FiveStarCengage
Visit our website—http://www.gale.cengage.com/fivestar
Contact Five Star Publishing at FiveStar@cengage.com

Printed in Mexico
Print Number: 01 Print Year: 2021

For Mary Skipper Long
Patient Wife, Fierce Mother, Trusted Advisor, Best Friend

Chapter One

I'm not what you'd call "handy." Problem is I'm right-handed, and by that, I mean right-handed only. See, a little south of Santa Fe, my left hand was shot off some years back.

I tell folks I'm one-handed, but my wife disputes me. She says I'm "one-and-one-quarter-handed," as I still have my left thumb intact. It's beyond me how she figures losing four fingers and most of my palm still leaves me with one fourth of a hand. Go add that up.

Could be because she's never known me any other way. One of the men who kidnapped her and used her badly had shot me in the left hand about three seconds after I first laid eyes on her. Then he did it again.

That was back around 1879, and I've had over eleven years to get pretty used to my claws. There's been several of them, garden variety, as they do rust and get bent. All that time, and I still manage to hook her clothes, tablecloths, furniture, and such.

"You are not very handy, Brodie Dent," she just said, right after I snagged her apron. Tore it.

I said, "Oh yeah? Come over here and try the other hand. And it's a small, small woman who'd mock a poor, defenseless cripple."

"Defenseless?" She snorted. "Against what, a herd of elephants?" She pulled off the apron and poked a finger through the latest hole. "Tell that defenseless story to all the men you shot or hauled off to jail."

"Well, I ain't never-ever had a defense against your tongue, you daggone fishwife. I'll get you a new apron. And I'll try to be more careful, Miz Emmalee Dent."

She tossed the apron in the rag box and jumped in my lap. "No fair being nice, Marshal."

She really is small. And really, really pretty, still, after all these years of hard times with me and her first husband. I really, really like her.

Just as the morning began to get interesting, here comes our adopted son, Wade, fifteen years of pent-up energy, busting in the kitchen side door.

"Whoa. Y'all want me to come back?" Big grin.

"No point," I said. "You done ruint it. What you got?"

Emmalee stood and straightened her dress, then slapped the back of my head.

"Mail," Wade said. "You got a durn letter."

Now, that's not something you hear every day in Mobeetie, Texas.

"It's from somebody name of Sentell." Wade grinned. "Know of him?"

Emmalee's knuckle went to her mouth. "Oh, Lord," she muttered.

I said, "Can't be good."

Wade handed me the envelope. "Aw, come on, Pop. You always have fun with Uncle Jack."

As usual, Curly Jack Sentell didn't waste words.

"Catch the train," he wrote. "Meet me and Squeak in Woodward, first week in Aug. Do you know somebody else can shoot, bring him. Or two. I'll pay. Selling a herd."

Emmalee let out a slow sigh of relief. "Woodward, over in the Indian Territory. Not so bad, then. Selling a herd. He's just looking for an escort back to the ranch. Don't you think so, Brodie?"

I nodded.

"Don't make sense, Mama Em. He'll have six or eight cowpokes who helped him with the trail up. Why'd he need more to get home?" Wade looked from me to Emmalee, but I could see he was already getting itchy.

I said, "He'll be packing a payoff coming home. Some of his men will take their pay and stay on in Woodward to blow it. Some is vaqueros and will take their stake to Mexico. Some can't be trusted. He might have ten, twelve thousand in cash after paying off the hands."

Wade got right to the itchy part. "So, who you gonna take?"

I gave Emmalee a sideways wink. "I was thinking on Seth Burton. Maybe Paco Ramirez."

Wade said, "Seth Burton's got a broke leg, Pop. I thought you knew that. And Paco moved to Amarillo. And you can't hardly take your deputy. Somebody's got to watch the town." He was coming right out of his skin.

"Guess I'll have to go it alone."

"Aw, now, Pop, that ain't right. You been saying you'd let me go next time the job wasn't so bad. This ain't no manhunt or nothing. All you need is a shotgun rider. I can do that."

Emmalee said, "He's messing with you, Son. Go pack. This letter is two weeks old. Y'all need to ride to Canadian tomorrow and catch that afternoon train." She tousled his hair.

"Hot damn!" he whooped as he headed for the ladder.

Emmalee whacked him harder than she'd hit me earlier. "Mouth!" she snapped.

"Yes'm, Mama Em. I'm sorry. But, I mean, hot damn!" He disappeared into the loft.

"It's time," she said. "He's near sixteen and as big as you. And he lives in awe of you and Curly Jack."

"You surprised?"

"Not at all, Brodie. But I think you miss my point. He is easily impressed. You two need to teach him more than just your infernal war stories while you're out gallivanting around."

"War stories?"

"You know perfectly well what I mean, Brodie. Your hero tales of daring feats. Yours and Curly's. I declare, they get better and farther from the truth each time you tell them. Do you forget that I was there for many of those incidents?" One hand on her hip, the other in my face.

"Well, no, I just . . ."

"And he thinks the two of you won the War of Rebellion for the South. It has somehow evaded him that you were about ten when the 'Civil War' ended."

"I never said . . ."

"And we won."

There was that again. I think a man should give it a lot of thought before marrying a damn Yankee. I don't care how much he loves her.

I was dog-assed tired as Wade and I saddled up the next morning. Emmalee had gone through one of her "frustration dream" nights. Which means so did I. She shook me awake the first time at around quarter past one.

"I was in this big mercantile, Brodie. Bigger than here. Like the ones in New Mexico Territory. Remember? They had everything."

"New Mexico?"

"Santa Fe, Brodie. And Las Vegas. Are you listening? It was as if I couldn't find anything. I was trying to get you and Wade ready for your trip. There was ham, but no skillet. Beans but no pot. Coffee but no water. One sock. No one would help me, and you were in such a rush. Hold me, Brodie. Don't let me slip back into it."

I held her and patted her back and pretended I cared for maybe ten minutes while she whimpered and muttered things I couldn't understand, then went under again. Until maybe two thirty.

"You don't care, do you? I can't get out of this, and you're snoring? I think I'm going crazy, Brodie. Everything is just out of my reach. Wade's boots are gone."

I rubbed my eyes and pulled her up under my arm again. "No, baby. You're just dreaming again. You . . ."

"I know that, Brodie. Help me get out of it. I close my eyes and slide right back into it. I want to scream."

"I do understand, Emmalee. I've had some like that. Like I'm not ready to travel. Got all my guns, but no cartridges. None. Horse is saddled, but no reins or belly band. Everyone's leaving but me."

"Are they nightmares, Brodie? Do they scare you?"

"No, Em. It's just worry. Frustration. Curly says it's trip anxiety, is all." I patted her back some more and tried to go back to sleep. Almost made it.

"Anxiety," she huffed. "I didn't realize he knew that word. Does Mister Sentell have these dreams too?"

"Curly Jack? You serious? Curly ain't anxious about nothing. He thinks I'm crazy. Says if you wake up 'cause you forgot something, get up and fix it and get back to sleep. Simple as that, he says."

I lay there thinking about Curly Jack. He could go through a running gun fight or stampede or sandstorm, pull up for the night, eat, and then go out like a blown candle in no time. Horse unsaddled, fed, watered, wiped down, and hobbled, and him out cold on the hard ground. With his lariat circled around him, to keep snakes away. And then wake up whenever he wanted to.

I realized there was this gentle humming beside me, fitful maybe but right steady. Emmalee's version of a snore. I looked at my watch on the bedside table. Held it up into the moonlight pouring through the window. Full moon. I should have known. Half past three. Sometime later I slid into the sleep of the dead.

At four she screamed, "No! Rawley, you come back here!"

That brought me upright and full awake. Rawley Byden was her first husband. A man she had shot dead many years back.

"Rawley," I mumbled. "You want him back?"

"He walked out," she sobbed. "He took your coat. I couldn't stop him. My pistol was empty."

"Jeez, Emmalee. It's August. Let him take it." What the hell. I was going to get up at five anyway. I swung sideways and put my feet on the floor.

Chapter Two

Wade and I got away by six, headed for the station at the little town of Canadian, around thirty miles north and east. A patrol of Ninth Cavalry buffalo soldiers rode with us a good ways, before they swung east to head for the Washita River over in Indian Territory.

As we parted ways, we heard the morning train miles west of us going "Whoo–whoo" down to Amarillo.

"What do they carry on the down trip?" Wade asked.

I said, "I ain't sure. Food and trade goods, I guess. Mail. A bunch of empty cattle cars."

Wade said, "Yeah. I heard a lot of cattle is starting to be shipped from Amarillo now. How come Curly don't do that?"

"It's near as far to Amarillo from the LT spread as it is to Woodward, and then you got to pay for more rail time. Plus, he fattens up the herd on the move north."

"Makes sense," Wade said. "Guess you need to show me on a map sometime. Any problem, us riding without them darky horse soldiers?"

"Naw," I said. "Long time since the Kiowa and Comanche were bad here. Now, fourteen years ago was different. There was two fights within ten miles of right here."

Wade said, "I remember. Uncle Curly told me about them. Buffalo wallow fight and the Lyman wagon train, right?"

"Yep. And now the cavalry patrols the cattle drives to keep the reservation Indians from stealing them blind. But we still pay attention, all around us."

"Yessir. And thanks for bringing me. And thanks for the guns."

I had given him a sawed-off ten-gauge double, my street gun. I also hung one of my big Colt double actions on his pommel. And a Remington .38 rimfire on his belt.

Me? I wore a cut-down Colt double action on my left side, cross draw; it was on a gunbelt hung on suspenders that Curly Jack had rigged for me, with my knife on the right side. The rig was easy to get in and out of, what with my missing hand and claw and all. There was another Colt in a pommel holster draped over my fancy saddle horn, and a '73 Winchester carbine in my scabbard. All my guns were .44-40's. You don't need to fool with different kinds of cartridges when you're shorthanded.

Wade gave me this look as we crossed the little stream that became the Washita River some distance to the east. "We do get chased into some buffalo hole, I won't be much help with pistols and a scattergun. Time I can hit 'em, they'd be on us."

"Maybe we find you a long gun in Canadian. If not, we'll get you something in Woodward."

"Didn't Curly use to push his herds up into Kansas? Dodge City, Wichita?"

I said, "Yep, you remember it right. Thing is, Kansas cut off any herds from Texas a while back, 'cause of Texas fever."

"That the same as tick fever?"

"It is. They is another name, too, which I disremember. Anyways, now we got this rail line coming through the territory from Kiowa, Kansas, and Woodward has become the new shipping point for a good part of Texas. I 'spect all the girls has fled south from Dodge, Wichita, and Hays, chasing those cowboy dollars."

"But ain't the cattle still being shipped into Kansas? You said the new line goes to Kiowa, right?"

"Right again. They is other connections there, so I'm told.

Seems it ain't a problem shipping Texas cattle through Kansas, long as they don't mingle with Kansas livestock. Their cattle can't stand up to tick fever, where ours ain't affected. They just carry it, and it don't mean you can't eat the meat."

Wade gave me that little grin of his. "Oh. I thought maybe we was just trying to poison Yankees."

We got in to Canadian by early afternoon, despite a normal Panhandle head wind.

I swear, it comes across the prairie so strong that you have to learn to walk upright again, every time you get out of it and go into some building.

Canadian hadn't changed much since my last visit, though I did notice two white dogs that were new. A little cluster of buildings just up the slope from the Canadian River, it was too small to be called a town, yet too big to be an anthill or even an outpost.

"Where to?" Wade asked.

"Trading store, that bigger building on your right. They sell guns when they got 'em. They don't sell liquor. Seems they frown on demon rum after some drunk buffalo soldiers up from Fort Elliot killed the former owner some years back. Over cards. They don't tolerate cards neither. You want strong drink or gambling whilst visiting this region, you got to go another few hundred yards across the river to Hog Town."

Only long gun for sale was a Sharps .50-70 carbine. I bought it along with twenty rounds.

"These are what we carried in the Ranger Frontier Battalion, back in the seventies. Clunky old single shot, but it'll knock down anything you hit. We'll try and trade it for something slicker in Woodward. I could use a beer. Let's cross over to Hog Town and get us something to eat. And drink."

"Uncle Curly told me about Hog Town, too. Is that all we're

going to get? Food?" Another durn grin.

"You better hope so."

We swung down and tied off in front of the cantina. As we started in, one of the working girls hailed us from a dugout across the road. Heavyset brute of a lady, mustache better than mine.

"Hello, boys. Come visit with Penny. I'll give you something you never had before. French delights."

Wade stared. I shoved him toward the door.

"She for real? What's she talking about?"

"That's Penny Choteau. Cajun queen. She's probably talking about the bloody flux. You ain't had that yet, have you?"

Inside, a gambler with an English accent laughed and said, "Penny Dreadful couldn't entice you into her parlor?"

I smiled back. "Not one single chance in hell. What's our best bet for grub?"

"Carne asada, if pork is acceptable."

Wade whispered. "Asada is beef. I know that for a fact."

I grinned at him. "Not here. Not today. Hell, this is Hog Town. The gambler was only letting us know. Leastways it ain't dog."

"You sure?"

"Not exactly."

We finished the so-called carne asada and washed it down with a small bucket of beer. I tossed some coins on the table and pushed off the nail keg that passed for a chair. The gambler caught my eye.

He said, "I trust it suited you, Marshal?" Had this little half smile. Friendly kind, though. Not snotty nor snooty.

I smiled back and said, "Tolerable."

"Good, then. Most excellent," he said. "You aren't likely to shoot me for bad advice. Or worse yet, incarcerate me in this

God-forsaken village."

"I ain't either displeased or on duty, so you're safe for the moment. Now, you don't like this place, how come you're here? And what makes you think I'm the law?" I was wearing my badge, but it was under my vest.

"The hook begins to give you away, and your answer confirms it. 'Not on duty,' you said. But who hasn't heard of Brodie Dent, marshal of Mobeetie? A man who has single-handedly, so to speak, kept the peace in the Panhandle for years? And who has cut down scores of wrong-doers in the process, yet who is not without scars himself."

Wade stood and butted in. "It ain't been scores that he's shot. Maybe eight or ten. And he's been winged a time or two, but he's still upright. Them others ain't. Is he mocking you, Pop?"

The gambler placed both hands in front of him, palms out, and raised his eyebrows at me.

I said, "And you holding a ten-gauge? Not likely. You're a mite prickly, Son. Maybe overly so." As I spoke I eased the barrels of Wade's shotgun down toward the floor.

"Friendly conversation among men," said the gambler. "Nothing more."

"All well and good," Wade said, "but Mama Em said men was always looking to be the one who killed Brodie Dent." He kept his eyes on the gambler and his thumb on one hammer of that shotgun. "She didn't say that they weren't no foreigners interested. And you still ain't said why it is you're here, Mister Duke of England."

The gambler grinned, showing us a gold tooth. "Let's begin again. I am James Abernathy, Earl of Rotting Ham and Lord of Nothingness. I am known far and wide as Jim. I am currently an unemployed gambler, arriving this very morning from lovely provincial Tascosa, and awaiting the train to Woodward. Where I perhaps will become employed again."

Wade said, "Unh-hunh." Way he said it was at least more open and accepting than he'd sounded before.

I said, "That's it?"

Jim gave me a shrewd look. "You are not also some federal lawman, are you? Do you have jurisdiction in the Indian Territory?"

"Strictly local."

"Well, then. There was some difficulty in Tascosa, and there is a man I hope to find in Woodward. To kill him. And you, gentlemen? Are you coming or going?"

"Heading for Woodward our own selves. Meeting an old friend who might need an escort back to Texas. Curly Jack Sentell."

The gambler got sort of a shrewd look. "Payroll, perhaps? I believe he is some sort of a cattle baron, from down along the Red River."

I decided I might better watch my mouth. And him. I said, "No payroll." That was true. "He sent word for us to come, so here we go."

"Truly a good friend, then. Didn't I hear you used to ride with him? Or perhaps for him?"

I said, "For him, mostly. I was his deputy, after I left the Rangers. Where did you learn so much about us?"

"About you, for the most part. And in Tascosa. You had a rather glorious gun fight there with a Negro soldier, did you not? Many years ago? It is still a local legend."

"Glorious, my sweet ass," I said. "He was a deserter, and he come at me shooting, in a durn alley. I had to kill him."

All right, it weren't quite that simple. I was still a Ranger then and rode with a sergeant from Fort Elliot to chase down this darky who had cut somebody and stole a U.S. horse. The sergeant went into this bar to get him, whilst I waited in the alley by the side door. The soldier come busting out almost on top of me with a Richards Colt in hand, and we opened up on one another. His first shot nicked my lower leg and brought me low, which is probably why he missed high with his last four shots. What with me shooting back there was so much smoke we couldn't hardly see each other. I got off four shots and only hit him with three, but they was sufficient.

"I heard there was more to it. Were you not wounded?"

"He winged me. Chipped my leg bone, which was right where it broke when I got thrown in Sweetwater, some time later. Put me out of the Rangers."

"Sweetwater?"

I said, "It's what Mobeetie used to be named."

Behind me the bartender said, "There's that train whistle. Right on time. Y'all best skedaddle."

The Canadian River was low enough that we could cross it at a lope. We were at the water tank that marked the train stop for Canadian in plenty good time. The gambler rode with us.

The train chugged in slow, towing a long line of full cattle cars. Between them and the engine and tender were two horse cars, a passenger car, and the baggage car.

I said, "If you two will get the horses loaded, I'll take the long guns and wait at the steps to the passenger car."

The gambler said, "I don't have a long gun."

"Well, you can tote Wade's shotgun 'til we get to Woodward. I just bought him an old carbine."

"You expecting trouble, Marshal?"

"Well, Lord Jim, I might as well be. It seems to find me whether I'm looking for it or not."

He took my reins and gave me that gold-tooth smile again. "Lord Jim. That's new. I think I like it."

Chapter Three

At the steps to the passenger car, Lord Jim took the shotgun from me and cracked the breech to check the loads.

"Buckshot, I presume?"

I nodded. "Double-aught, if it please Your Majesty."

He laughed. "I'll be well pleased if I don't have to fire this cannon. Now, we may find seating a bit tight in here."

"Yeah?"

Wade pulled himself up the steps. "He's right, Pop. Both horse cars was near full."

Only good news inside was there were actual seats, some facing each other, instead of long benches. It was smoky, smelly, and hot as all hell. Main problem was I couldn't make out but maybe five empty seats, and none of them were together.

I said, "Bad luck. I'd hoped to ask you about Tascosa while we eat smoke."

There was one open seat in the last section by the back steps.

Lord Jim spoke to the three men sitting there. "Would two of you consider taking other seats so that we might discuss business?"

One, a cavalry corporal, said nothing but moved to another empty seat. The other two didn't even look up.

Wade said, "Y'all go on and set here. I'll grab a seat by myself. Y'all can talk."

Lord Jim said, "Hold a moment, Wade. I don't believe these gentlemen heard me."

One of the gentlemen was a bleary-eyed cowpuncher, and the other looked to be a salesman. Derby hat, sample case, and dark suit.

The salesman said, "I heard you. I'm comfortable right here."

The cowboy said, "I ain't moving to suit no foreigner."

Lord Jim said, "The thing is, though, despite your feelings, Marshal Dent here would like to sit with me and his son."

Both men went wide eyed, looked at my claw, and then pushed by us to find other seats, muttering apologies.

The steam whistle screamed, and the train lurched and shuddered into motion. Engine smoke quickly overcame the cigar smoke. Wade and I pulled up our bandannas, while Lord Jim held a silk handkerchief over his nose and mouth. We were all soaked in sweat by the time the conductor came back from the baggage car to collect our fares.

Twenty minutes later the wind shifted to come at us from the west. Sent the smoke streaming away to our right and actually cooled us down a mite.

I pulled down my scarf and said, "You care to share what happened in Tascosa to get your blood up so?"

Lord Jim tucked his handkerchief in an inside vest pocket and said, "I don't mind. There's a young man there I grew fond of. He was a deputy, but he also worked with the blacksmith. Married the blacksmith's daughter, a deaf Mexican girl. Some thought him to be simple because his speech was somewhat impaired. He wasn't, not one bit."

I said, "You are right about that."

"Ah, you know him." He snapped his fingers. "Of course, you do. Your claw. I should have guessed. You see, that's what the trouble was about."

Wade said, "You're talking about Billy. He was the one who came up with Pop's hook, back when Pop got his hand shot off. They was all together then, Billy and Uncle Curly Jack, Pop, and even Mama Em. Right, Pop?"

I nodded. "Get on with the trouble part."

Lord Jim said, "Well then, you know Billy has built up a pretty good business in new parts for people. Artificial arms, claw hands, legs. People keep shedding pieces and coming to Blacksmith Billy for help. Like you."

"I do know that. He's replaced mine three times. Each time better. And?"

"And a lawyer showed up with a writ while I visited Santa Fe. A cease and desist writ. He showed Billy some papers claiming a patent on artificial limbs for some St. Louis company, then confiscated all Billy's stock of parts. He had a hired constable hold Billy at gunpoint while they loaded his parts and tools in a wagon and hauled them away."

I said, "Was Billy hurt?"

"Not so much. Roughed him and the old blacksmith up a bit, threatened the wife, but they are all right, physically. Business-wise, Billy's ruined. They ransacked the house and also took his money and guns. Said they were going to Woodward to get a federal marshal to come back with them and sell the blacksmith shop at auction, because the tools and parts were made there."

Wade said, "What's a patent?"

I said, "It's a right, give by a court, to build something a certain way. Stops others from copying you or stealing your ideas."

"Like when Smith and Wesson shut down a bunch of gun makers for copying their cylinders," Wade said. "Uncle Curly told me about that. I wish I knew more about the law."

I laughed. "I wish you did, too. Might be you could keep us halfway straight." I turned to Lord Jim. "Do you think this was a legal action?"

"Not for a minute, I don't. Even if it was, that won't save

that shyster's life if I find him. No, this was pure fear and intimidation. He gets away with it in small towns, I'll wager, with no force of law behind his claims. I mean to stop him for good."

"Why? I mean, I'm all for settling this man's hash, but what's Billy to you?"

"A few months back I cleaned out a freighter in Tascosa at the table. He left, then slipped back in a side door and came at my back with a meat cleaver. I never even heard him. There was a gunshot and crash. Behind me was Billy with that sawed-off Colt and the dead freighter all in a jumble with half his head gone. The cleaver was buried in the floor boards, mere feet behind my chair. I owe Billy. And I've little use for the legal profession. Barristers, attorneys, judges—they're all cut from the same bolt of cloth."

He went on. "The thing is, I'm not proposing legal action against these men. I hate so-called legal action and legal actors. I mean to simply eliminate them." Jim's voice rose now. "They are parasites, preying on small successful businesses to take over or milk for money. There was probably no patent for Billy to infringe upon. They took Billy's drawings to prepare some patents themselves, to sell or to block small potatoes like Billy."

I said, "But you're right. Billy is small. How did they ever learn about him?"

"I heard of him long before I came to Tascosa," Jim said. "He has put artificial limbs on a remarkable number of people."

I said, "Well, that's a fact. Billy has got himself a reputation."

Jim nodded. "I've seen it before, both here and back in England. There you are, a hard-working, nice sort of fellow, the thoughtful type, a natural engineer. You design a better hay-baling machine, just to help your old dad on the family farm. Or perhaps a more efficient saw for your uncle's lumber mill. A new blasting cap . . . whatever. You do well for a while, but then word spreads, and first thing you know, here comes a bloody lawyer for some big company. Maybe they buy you out, but if you are without representation, more often than not they roll over you like a steam engine. Bogus patents, legal gobbledygook, and such."

Wade said, "Representation?"

Jim said, "It means, do you have a lawyer to represent you. One you trust, if such a thing exists."

I snorted. "Billy ain't big enough for a lawyer, honest or not."

"And that's exactly who these shysters look for. Vermin. They need to be exterminated like wharf rats."

Wade looked somewhat confused then, so I said, "He means wiping out the lawyers, Son." I turned to Jim. "But can you just shoot them?"

"It would be preferable if they start the engagement. Or appear to."

He liked to talk, but I liked listening to him. And I agreed with him about lawyers.

Wade nudged me. "I like to hear him talk, don't you? And he don't like lawyers no more'n you."

Lord Jim cocked his head slightly and said, "What's this, then? You've had your own legal dust-up?"

I shrugged. "You could say so. My wife and her first husband were sheepherders there in Tascosa and were doing all right until her and some Mex women were kidnapped and took to Santa Fe to be sold or rented. Me and Billy and her husband rode with Marshal Sentell to recover the women. I got my hand shot off in the process, but we got 'em home. Problem was her husband thought something happened 'tween me and her."

He smiled. "Seems as if it did."

"No, sir," I said. "No, siree, Bob. Not my fault, but she wasn't having none of that. Lot more happened, but, to cut this short, some time later he tried to kill me. And she killed him instead."

"And is that where the law came in?"

I said, "No, not right then. We married and had a pretty nice sheep ranch to run. Seemed set for life, except she couldn't have babies. About the time we adopted Wade here, her husband's family from Michigan sent a lawyer to take the ranch, the herd, and the house and sell it all. 'Wrongful death,' they claimed and put us out in the cold. Had a judge in their pocket. Another jumped-up lawyer. We moved to Mobeetie, and I put on the badge again."

Lord Jim said, "But you do all right, it appears. All those darky soldiers contribute to your comfort, do they?"

I laughed. "Fines and collections? The Fort Elliot troopers don't add much. Their sergeants generally keep them pretty straight. No, how we make it is that me and the missus own a part of a bar. It would be hard to live on fifty a month."

Wade said, "He still whacks a few rowdies every week. And fines 'em. They just usually ain't darkies."

Jim studied Wade for a moment. "And you're adopted. Where did they find a feisty piece of work like yourself? Ranging with a wolf pack? Riding a hairy buffalo across the plains?"

Wade darkened. "My folks died. Was kilt, anyways. I was pretty young, but I remember them." He got up and walked out on the back platform.

Jim said, "I touched upon a nerve."

"Yep," I said. "His daddy was a drinker and a hitter. Bull-whacker—what you might call a freighter. His momma come to my wife Emmalee one day with a black eye. The boy had a swoll-up ear. He was maybe nine years old. She asked Emmalee if she'd watch after the boy. Em didn't know she meant forever. Woman went back to their shack, poured coal oil on his drunken butt, then set the place ablaze. Some said they heard a gunshot or two as it went up, but anyways they both burned up in it."

"My Lord! Think of her despair."

"I guess she took all she could. Anyways, Wade's been with us ever since. Six years now."

Jim said, "I am certain he is better off."

I nodded. "It sure weren't no good like it was."

We chugged into Woodward late in the day. As the train groaned and wheezed to a stop we all stood and stretched.

"You've visited here before, I'll warrant." Lord Jim drew a bone-handled Colt conversion and topped it off with a sixth round as he spoke.

"Nope," I said. "You expecting to run into this lawyer on the loading dock?" Most folks who worked with revolvers let their hammer rest on an empty chamber, unless they figured trouble was nearabouts.

"I have yet to meet the gentleman. I have only his name and description, but I'll begin my search immediately and had best be ready." He shoved the revolver back in an underarm holster.

"I'd like to give you a hand, if you don't mind the company. Billy is right special to me, too. And if Curly Jack Sentell hears of this first, won't neither one of us get much of a chance at them two." I pulled my own revolver and added another cartridge to the cylinder.

"And why is that?"

"Billy's momma was a working girl and was Curly Jack's woman. She was murdered by that gang we chased to Santa Fe, years back. Billy ain't his son, but he might as well be."

"Well, Marshal Dent, what do you propose?"

"Why don't we take care of the horses, then grab a bath and some grub before we go man hunting." I put that out more as a plan than a question.

He said, "And young Wade?"

"I've been told we can eat at the Dew Drop Inn. I'll park Wade there when we hit the streets."

That was the plan. It lasted all the way until we stepped off the train.

Chapter Four

Curly Jack and Squeak were waiting on the platform. Wade spotted them as we waited to get off.

"How'd he know we'd be on this train, Pop?"

"Durned if I know, Son."

He spotted us then and yelled, "About dang time. I met ever' train for three days now."

We did some catching up and introduced Lord Jim, but as soon as Curly Jack heard what happened in Tascosa, everything changed.

"I know exactly who you're talking about. Seen 'em talking loud and drinking in the bar at Dew Drop Inn last night. Bragging about cleaning somebody out. If I'd had any idea they was talking about Billy and Conchita, they'd be dead or ruined right now."

Curly stopped for a minute and stared off like his mind was a thousand miles away. A porter pushed a handcart loaded with baggage right up to him and said, "How 'bout you ease outta my way, friend?"

Curly turned, and his eyes burned a hole right through that man. Didn't say a word. Didn't have to.

"I, uh, I'm sorry, Mister. I'll just take this around the other way." He scurried off.

Curly came back to the present. "Y'all can wait on your baths and grub. We'll get your mounts unloaded, and Squeak and

Wade can get them took care of. Us three will waltz over to the Dew Drop and settle this."

As we walked to the saloon, Curly said, "So, Abernathy, you seen all this. Will you swear to it?"

Lord Jim said, "Actually, I saw none of it but the aftermath. But it happened just as I said, and I will happily swear in any court that I saw it all."

Curly gave him a hard took, then said, "Good. Good man. Brodie, you still wear a badge?"

I said, "I do." I pulled open my vest and showed him.

"All right then, I'm giving you my spoken warrant for their arrest."

"Curly, you know I got no jurisdiction on a crime in Tascosa."

"It was a crime against a boy from Mobeetie. Your town. Besides which, this ain't gonna go to no trial."

I thought, *Oh, hell.* I said, "You right sure?"

"We fixing to defend ourselves, Brodie. I mean to give them a fair shake, but it is not gonna go smooth for the other side." He drew a Schofield and strode into the Dew Drop Inn. Lord Jim and I pulled our revolvers and followed him in.

The bar and eating area were off to one side of the hotel desk. We went straight there.

Curly said, "That's them, them two at that back table. You mark 'em?"

I said, "Slick Easterner and bushy-whiskered fat man?"

"They was the ones I heard," Curly said.

Lord Jim said, "They are as Billy described them. Pork-pie hat on one and the beard of the other. You might ask if the slick one is named Iverson."

I said, "And ask to see his patents."

Curly said, "Why?"

"If they do have them and a big company behind them, we kill them, and their company comes right back at us with federal marshals and warrants. Billy's worse off, and we're on the run. Now, if they're shy on patents, they're clear-cut thieves, and we got no legal problem shooting them."

Jim said, "There would be no problem for me either way. Just let me walk over there and shoot them. I'll swear it was self-defense, if anyone here even cares."

Curly said, "No, sir, that boy they robbed is family. Up to me and Brodie to make it right." He nodded toward the bartender, then started for the back table. I was thinking, *family*?

Jim strolled to the bar, pistol along his thigh, and smiled at the burly man behind it. I heard Jim say in a low voice, "We're just going to observe what happens next, are we not?"

The bartender nodded and placed both hands on the bar. I moved up beside Curly as he confronted the two seated men.

"Iverson? Fresh in from Tascosa, right?" Curly wore a disarming smile.

I was wired tight as Dick's hatband, but it was something to watch their faces as they looked at our faces, then my claw, then our pistols.

"Who's asking?" said Whiskers. Slick had gone right pale.

"That was my stepson you robbed. Let's go collect the money and stuff you took offen them nice people, and I'll put you on the next train going east."

"Y—you can't do this," stuttered the lawyer. "I'm an attorney at law, and this man is my licensed constable."

"Here's the thing, Slick. Y'all are gonna be on that train. Question is if you're in coffins or not." Curly cocked his pistol, so I did, too. "Now show me some legal papers."

Seems like those clicks set off Whiskers. He pushed back and tried to draw and stand, but I put one in his chest, and he went down in a tangle with his chair. Started gurgling up blood. I've shot some folks over the years, but it never fails to run my heart right up in my throat. And the blast and flame from a sawed-off forty-four forty will startle the hell out of you every time, even if it's you pulling the trigger.

I stepped into the gun smoke and kicked his pistol away, but, to tell the truth, he didn't seem as if he'd be with us long.

Slick froze.

I said, "Show us some patents on spare parts. You know, for people."

He said, "I don't have any. I mean, not here. Not with me."

Curly said, "You armed, Slick?"

The lawyer nodded his head, real slow.

Curly sort of startled me then. He said, "Good. Go on and pull it out. Lemme just see it." As the lawyer began to draw a small open-top Colt from his vest, Curly shot him, right in the head. Killed him dead as a red brick. Whiskers coughed once and quit breathing right then, too.

Curly bent and retrieved the pistol from the dead lawyer. "Coffins it is, then."

We re-holstered and knelt to search the bodies. I was only half aware of a man in a dark suit coming in the back door. From the privy, I figured. Probably right, too, but then I remembered there were three plates on that table. Hair on my neck stood up, and Lord Jim yelled, "Look out!"

I saw a nickel-plated Colt coming from under that dark coat. I shoved Curly over and dove away as the gunfire started again. Three shots. I was sure I was hit in the left hip, but through the smoke I saw the stranger jerk twice, drop his pistol, and then fall sideways against the piano. He slumped to a sitting position, staring at the blood on his chest.

Lord Jim marched over to him, pistol cocked and aimed at his head. "Who are you? What's all this to you?"

The stranger groaned. "I'm his employer." He nodded at

Slick. "I'm from St. Louis."

Lord Jim said, "So, this was all your doing."

"I don't know what you mean," the man wheezed. "I'm shot. I need help. This hurts."

Lord Jim said, "This will have to do" and shot him in the forehead.

My heart was barely out of my throat from my own shooting, and I was still half in shock from Curly blasting Slick. I said, "Good Lord, Jim!"

He shrugged. "Ah, well. He was dying anyway, wasn't he now?"

Curly Jack nodded approval. He wasn't much on forgiveness, even less so for someone who hurt a friend. And God help you if you hurt family. And Curly decided who was family.

The desk clerk had seen it all. One glance at my badge, and he was happy to take us up to the rooms of the newly departed.

We cleaned out the money and guns. There was right much cash, as they had sold all of Billy's gear and spare parts. Curly Jack gave the desk clerk more than enough to get the three scoundrels all set in coffins and on their way to an address in St. Louis, which came off a card in Slick's room. The desk clerk seemed eager to help. Curly Jack affects most folks that way. As we walked out, the clerk said, "They had a wagon they was trying to sell, too."

I really didn't want to irritate Curly, but I had to ask. "How come we don't just bury them here?"

"Well, Brodie, I mean to send them buggers in St. Louis a message."

Turned out that lick on my left hip was a slug bouncing off my Colt. It didn't seem any worse for wear, though my holster was torn up, and I had a bruise the size of my hand under the pistol.

"Likely knocked your pistol out of timing," Curly said. "We'll go by Rath's store and let his gunsmith look it over. Iffen it's ruint we can pick up a fresh one right there."

"That's good," I said. "I need to trade Wade's Sharps for a repeater, anyways."

Lord Jim said, "Do I understand you plan to return Billy's guns and money to Tascosa?"

Curly glanced at me. "I know you'd do it for me, Brodie, but I'd kinda like to see Billy and Conchita my own self. Ain't that far outta my way."

"It is way out of your way," I said, "but me and Wade will ride along and then see you back to your ranch once you're done visiting."

Curly shrugged, and Lord Jim said, "In that case I'd beg to accompany you as far as Tascosa. And I don't have a long gun. Could I buy that Sharps? It appears simple enough even for an untrained gambling man."

Me and Lord Jim cut a deal on the Sharps, and I told him if he found something better in Rath's store I'd let him off the hook. That didn't happen.

Rath's gunsmith showed me my Colt wouldn't fire on double action. Said he could probably get it back in timing if I left it.

Curly said, "Told you, Brodie. Good thing we checked." To the gunsmith he said, "We ain't got time to wait for it, Smitty. You got another self-cocker we can trade him up to?"

Smitty said, "In fact I do. Better one, to my way of thinking. These new Smith and Wessons are real trigger-cockers. You can bring 'em to full cock with a trigger squeeze right up 'til you meet resistance. Hold it there 'til you take aim, then touch it off with just a tad more pressure. It's a break-top, sorta like your friend's Schofield. Faster to reload. And easier." He nodded at my claw, like I might not of thought about that. "Try this one. It's a forty-four Russian."

I did. Took me a couple of tries to get the squeeze right, but then it was like natural. I said, "I'm partial to forty-four forty caliber. You got one like that?"

He said, "The Frontier model. I got one left, but it's only a four-inch barrel."

I said, "Ideal. I'll need a holster, too. You got a Winchester carbine, same caliber?"

"I do not. Three rifles, no carbines. What I do have is this little Colt slide-action carbine to match your pistol. That hook of yours, you might like this better than a lever action. This one is called a Baby Lightning. A side-loader, just like your Winchester."

He was right again. My claw fit that slide near perfect, and I could pump it slicker than goose droppings. I gave Wade my Winchester, and we settled up on the guns and started looking around to see what we might need for the trip back to Texas.

The gunsmith eased up to me and said in a low voice, "I heard about your little scrape."

"Why you whispering?" I said.

"They is others in the store might run to the law. Marshal is out with a posse, but his deputy come by, maybe a half hour before y'all come in. He's looking for you."

I said, "So? He gonna be a problem for us?"

Curly Jack said, "Spit it out, Smitty."

Smitty looked at me. "I seen your badge. I ain't seen nothing on your two friends. Thing is, ain't no one supposed to be carrying guns here, less they's the law or fixing to leave."

I said, "We're just getting set to go."

Curly said, "It don't make sense. I been here most of a week, carrying the whole time."

Smitty said, "The deputy knows you, Curly. Hell, everybody knows you. You was hanging around the train station, so he figgered you was leaving. Main thing is he was shy about asking you to shuck 'em."

I said, "What changed?"

"He got a wire from the marshal, said he's on the train from Kioway tomorrow. Y'all done killed three men, so the deputy knows he's got to do something. Anything. Make a show."

I flicked my thumb at Curly and Lord Jim. "You see him, you tell him I deputized these two before the fight, and I had a warrant for two of them men. They resisted, and the third one bounced that bullet off my hip, making him an attempted murderer. Desk clerk in the Dew Drop seen it all. You think that marshal will come after us?"

Smitty said, "They been gone a week. They'll be tired, all of 'em. And this marshal, he's open to, uh, suggestions. Encouragement . . . you know what I mean?"

Curly said, "Think he'd be interested in a wagon?"

"I think that would convince him of your total righteousness. Would y'all be interested in a couple of old badges? I keep some for sale. Easterners love 'em. A quarter a piece. Heck, just take 'em. I'll take a commission on that wagon."

I took four. Gave two to Curly for him and Squeak, one to Lord Jim, and held one for Wade.

Curly said, "Let's swing by my chuck wagon, out back of the livery. Squeak and your boy will be there scaring up something to eat. I need to get Squeak and Cookie ready to roll out towards home come morning, along with a few cowpokes, my wrangler, and the remuda."

I said, "So, Squeak ain't riding the train with us?"

"Naw. He's got a nice little packet of cash for my missus. I'll keep the main stash with me."

"How nice? How little?"

"I sent her a thousand."

Chapter Five

Next morning it was drizzling, and, even though it weren't cold, that wind down from Kansas made us right miserable, driving that little bit of rain sideways and right under our hat brims and down our necks. All that dust turned to mud.

We huddled on the downwind side of Curly's chuck wagon and ate breakfast upright. Ham, bacon, eggs, biscuits, and coffee, with beans and peppers for them as wanted such.

Curly said, "You done good, Cookie. Where's Squeak?"

Curly's Mex cook poured more coffee and said, "I don't know."

Curly said, "You don't know nothing, or you don't know where he is?"

"I dunno where he is, Señor Boss. He don't say. You asked me where he is. Sure, I know something."

Curly exploded. "Well, consarn it, Cookie, what is it you know?"

"Señor Squeak, he see some old compadres last night. He say he has to go somewhere with them. He catch me on the trail, he say."

"What did he have to do with them?"

"He don't say that, too."

Wade came back from the depot just then to tell us the Amarillo train was delayed a few hours.

Curly snorted. "Well, ain't things just grand today? Cookie, soon as you feed Wade, you and the boys head out home. Maybe

Squeak will be back by then, but don't you wait for him. Rest of us will go wait in the Dew Drop for that durn train. I'll see you at the ranch in two or three weeks."

The rain got worse as we clattered along the boardwalks between the stables and the saloon. I thought it could be why their town lawmen never came around to bother us. Curly said as much, after we sat in the bar a while.

"Could be," I said. "Could be we're too heavy armed for them. Speaking of which, tell me about your new main gun there, Curly. Another Winchester?"

"It surely is." He unshucked it from its scabbard and handed it to me. It had a carbine butt and a saddle ring, maybe a twenty-two-inch barrel, but was full stocked like a musket. And hefty.

"Kinda hefty," I said.

"Needs to be," he said. "It's a .50-95. She kicks like a fornicating mule, even as heavy as she is. Action is a good bit stronger than a '76 Winchester. This one is a model '86."

"So, you finally retired Sally Ann?" Sally Ann was a '76 rifle in .45-75 caliber and had been Curly's long gun for over ten years.

"She's still a fine shooter and hangs over my fireplace. But she won't touch this one for damage. This one kills at both ends. I call her Sally Sue."

Wade whistled. ".50-95? That's even more punch than that Sharps Lord Jim is toting. Lots more."

Lord Jim smiled. "I expect it would suffice for elk or buffalo, Curly, would it not?"

Curly nodded. "Or grizzlies. Or brick walls." He slid it back in its scabbard.

The train from Kiowa finally chugged in around noon, just as the rain got worse. We stood in the downpour by the horse car, watching as the scraggly local posse unloaded their mounts and trudged off into the gloom, pushing one prisoner. Probably fixing to look for us.

Didn't take us long to load up and get seated, and of course the durn rain quit as soon we got aboard. As we pulled away from Woodward, I thought how Curly's luck still held up pretty good. Or maybe it was my good luck. I surely didn't need to get mixed up in some no-win showdown of strong wills between Curly Jack Sentell and some young lawman needing to prove who's boss. I already knew whose side I'd come down on. Wasn't necessarily on the side of the law.

The passenger car wasn't nearly as crowded as it had been on the trip up. Besides the four of us there was a skinny salesman sitting with a burly bald man, who turned out to be the foreman of a clutch of six Chinee railroad workers. The Chinee sat in the back corner and chattered away, passing a long-stemmed pipe.

There was also a darky soldier, a corporal, going to rejoin the Tenth Cavalry, somewheres down south. Last was a scrawny female teacher with two kids, heading for Amarillo. Didn't none of them appear to be armed, excepting the corporal, who wore his long-barreled Colt.

We learned all that in the first hour from Wade, who went around and talked with each of them. Well, he spoke to the six Chinee, but they didn't have much English between them, so they just smiled and nodded.

And our firepower drew some concerned stares from the others, as did my claw, but Wade calmed them by saying we was lawmen traveling home. He even showed his badge.

After a bit the corporal went to the privy at the back end of the car, then stopped alongside me on the way back to his seat.

He touched his hat brim to Curly, then nodded toward my claw.

"You the law, up to Mobeetie, ain't you?"

I nodded.

"I seen you there, some years back. You expecting trouble, Marshal? All them guns? See, I left my carbine in the scabbard on my saddle, but I kin surely climb in the horse car and get it, do you think I need to."

I smiled. "I expect we all coulda left our long guns on the horses, same as you. Who's going to mess with an empty cattle train heading south, anyways?"

"Yassuh, Mister Marshal, I believe you's right. I'm gonna get some sleep."

Me and my big mouth. Wasn't much later the brakes screamed, and half of us was thrown forward out of our seats.

Chapter Six

We had just dropped down into a shallow valley alongside a near-dry creek bed, when we screeched to a stop. The tracks were in a long slow curve to the right, so we could see the problem, easy enough. Up ahead, one of the rails was pried loose and angled down toward the creek.

Curly said, "Whoever did this weren't trying to wreck us. Tore up the track where we could see it with plenty of time to stop."

The corporal said, "Yassuh. They just wanted us to stop right here."

Curly whipped around to peer out the left-side windows.

"They'll come at us from up there, top of the ridge," he said. To the passengers he yelled, "If you ain't armed, get on the floor! Rest of you, don't shoot less I say to. I wanna see how many they is. Stay low, and stay put."

Lord Jim said, "Perhaps you non-combatants would do well to get under the seats on the right side. And do *not* poke your heads up to see what's happening. We'll tell you when it's safe."

Curly said, "Good. Y'all do it now. I'm gonna yell at the engineer. Corporal, why don't you borrow the marshal's shotgun and slip back and set up in the caboose, 'case they try to run up our tail end."

It wasn't a question, and the corporal didn't take it that way. Wade handed him the ten-gauge and the bandolier of shells, and, poof, the trooper was out the back door and gone, just as

Curly went out the front. I could hear Curly and the engineer and fireman yelling at each other but couldn't make out all they said over the chuffing and whooshing of the engine.

Directly Curly was back and said, "They got two pistols up there. I tole 'em to stay low and don't shoot, less they was set upon. Any sign from up the ridge?"

"Nary a trace," I said. "You think maybe they ain't nobody up there?"

There was a boom and a puff of smoke from uphill, and a bullet spanged off the engine, all sort of right together.

"No, Brodie, I don't think they ain't up there. I'd say up there is exactly where they is. Hold fire."

There was another boom, and a bullet thudded into the roof of our car.

Curly yelled uphill, "Y'all hold fire! We got women and children in here. What is it you want?"

It was quiet for a few seconds. Curly yelled again. "Can you assholes even speak English!?"

"We speak English!" somebody yelled back. "How many women?"

"Only one old teacher, and we won't give her up."

"I am not that old," the teacher protested. "I am not yet thirty."

"You wanna make it to thirty, you stay quiet," Curly hissed at her. "Them wanting money is bad enough, but if they is a woman in the deal, that's a whole nuther beehive."

"Your money or your lives!" some bandit shouted. "We know they's some cash from cattle sales on board."

"And how'd you know that, exactly?"

"We know. And that's all you needs to know, too."

Curly looked over at me. "You reckon that little peckerhead Squeak ran off at the mouth in Woodward?"

"Either that or he's with them."

Curly said, "No way. That boy wouldn't turn on me. If he's with 'em, they took him."

Somebody uphill yelled, "Well? We ain't got all night!"

Curly shouted back, "Tell you what. We're just gonna start backing up outta here. Y'all feel free to just ride in alongside us and try to take it!"

"Hold on! Hold on just a dang minute now."

Curly yelled back, "We ain't got all night!"

"Here's the thing, Mister Sentell. We got your boy Squeak, and we got dynamite. You try backing out, we'll go blow the track behind you. You don't give over that money, we got a breed who'll flay your boy alive. And come full dark, we'll slip down there and dynamite y'all and the whole train, one car at a time. And then I'll make me a pouch from your boy's skin."

Curly muttered, "Hmm."

Clearly, that meant he was studying on it. That pleased me to no end, as I couldn't see our way out, no way at all.

Squeak yelled out, "He'll do it, Curly! He means it. He'll flay me. Sweet Jesus, Curly, don't let him skin me! I'll work it off. Promise."

The bandit followed up with, "You push that around yor plate a while, old man. You ain't got to swallow it all at once, but you do got to choke it down."

Curly turned and sat on the floor, his back toward the bandits. He took off his hat, rubbed his face with his left hand, then gave me this shrewd look.

"Thing is, Brodie, I'm dead certain Squeak is in on this. He ain't ever called me nothing but 'boss.' And they ain't many of 'em or they'd be shooting us up. Anybody seen any of 'em? No? See what I'm saying?"

I said, "I do, Curly, but what about the dynamite?"

"They prob'ly ain't got none, but, if they do, you can bet dollars against cow chips they done sent somebody to blow that track behind us. No, that ain't the way out." He turned to the railroad man. "Look out the side at the damage they done up ahead. Go ahead. Stick your head up. They ain't gonna shoot. They's pretty dang certain they's about to get their way."

The railroad foreman peered ahead at the track. "I see it just fine," he said.

"That rail ain't bent, is it?"

He looked again. "No, sir. Pulled loose and away is all. Hellfire, they'da had to heat it up pretty good to bend it. Why?"

"How long would it take you and them Chinks to put it right if they weren't no one shooting at you? I mean, y'all got spikes and sledge hammers and such?"

"Our stuff is in the baggage car. Hell, we could put that rail back in place in a few minutes if they weren't nobody shooting at us."

Curly said, "They'll try shooting, but we gonna do our level best to pin 'em down. They ain't much as shooters, else they'd 'a done killed our engineer. Tell your Chinks I'll pay 'em a bonus, depending on how fast they get us rolling."

The foreman started talking monkey talk to one of the Chinee men. His Number Two, I guess.

Curly said, "I'm gonna try and buy us a little time, get us closer to dark." He rolled onto his knees and yelled out, "All right, you win! How you want the transfer?"

After a bit, the bandit shouted, "Put the money in a satchel and toss it out! Y'all back up a little ways down the track. Once we count it, we'll turn loose Squeak, uh, your boy. Y'all can back on up to Woodward, or stick around and fix the track. We'll be long gone."

Curly yelled back. "No, sir! No, siree Bob. I ain't leaving without my boy Squeak. I'll pledge my word not to shoot. You send him down here with your man to collect my cash. Soon as he's safe on board, we'll start backing away. You ask Squeak.

He'll tell you my word is good."

Curly said to me, "Dump the stuff outta my satchel and get ready to throw it out. Wade, ease on out and go tell that engineer to be ready to roll forward soon as them Chinks fix the track. You better stay there and help us lay down covering fire once we start."

Wade was gone in a flash.

I said, "You're pretty free with my family, ain't you?"

"He can get on and off better'n you is all, else I'd 'a sent you. Go holler at him to stay down if you're gonna fret over him."

The foreman said, "What about us? When do we grab our gear?"

Curly said, "Just hang on to your horses, Son. I got it covered." Uphill he yelled, "I'm sending men to get the money from the baggage car. Don't be shooting at 'em, you hear?"

The bandit roared back, "We hear! Go ahead on." He sounded right satisfied with himself.

Curly nodded to the foreman, and him and the Chinee men jumped off the train on the downhill side and ran to the baggage car.

Things had turned and seemed to be going just great, right up to then.

Then is when the baggage master told that foreman that he couldn't open up the car while the train was under attack. Jumping Jehoshaphat Christmas.

The Chinee men were hopping and yelling, and their foreman used some language I'm not sure I understood, even though it seemed like English.

Curly swung down, walked to the car, and said, "I'm Curly Jack Sentell. Do you know me?"

The baggage clerk came back weak. "Everybody knows you, Mister Sentell."

"Then you know if I say that I will break in there and kill you and rip off your cojones if you don't open this door *right now,* that is what I'll do. Don't you? Don't you know that?"

There was a click and a clang, and the door slid open. The plan was on again.

Chapter Seven

The bandit chief yelled, "Your man says we can trust you, but I won't send him down 'til we have the loot and count it! We send your man down, you might shoot our man, grab the money, and try to run. That don't work for me. You just throw it out, and, soon as we got it, we'll cut your boy loose, and y'all can be on your way."

Curly shouted back, "I don't see as I have much choice. Here's the money!" He stepped on the platform and slung the satchel out about twenty paces.

"You ain't gonna shoot? Not none of you?"

"Cross my heart!" Curly yelled back.

One of the bandits came over the hill at a gallop and raced down to pick up the satchel. He had to dismount to grab it. He started to remount, then looked inside.

"It's empty," he said, looking at us. He turned back uphill and yelled, "Durn thing is empty!" He stood there looking right stupid.

"Get back up here!" their boss yelled.

I heard Squeak shout at Curly, "You gave your word to pay up! You crossed your durn heart!"

Curly said, "Never said, 'Hope to die,' did I, you little back-stabbing pissant. And my fingers was crossed, too." He shot the pick-up man as he tried to remount. Knocked him and his pony down. Sounded like a daggone cannon.

"Get them Chinks to work!" Curly yelled. "Let's give 'em

some cover."

Me and Lord Jim started banging away at the ridge line. Pretty soon that trooper in the caboose started spraying them with buckshot, too. Probably not much effect at seventy yards, but blue whistlers will still cause a man to duck.

There weren't much return fire coming from uphill, if there was any at all. I was shucking that slide-action Colt carbine fast as you please, and Curly was working his big Winchester steady, too. Pretty soon we eased up to top off our carbines and let the smoke clear up some. It was blowing uphill, which was a small blessing itself. Just then Wade started firing from the cab. Thank you, Lord, I thought. Then I heard them Chinee men pounding them spikes.

I swear to you on my Momma's Bible, the sound they made was, "chink, chink, chink." I near about giggled, but then some bandit yelled, "Hey! They's fixing the track!"

We poured it on again. In no time, Wade shouted, "We're rolling!" and I felt the train shudder and start lurching forward.

There was some bangs and clanks as the Chinee men tossed in their tools and clambered back in our car.

"Brodie, let's you and me head for the caboose and help that corporal keep 'em off our back end."

As the train picked up speed, Curly stepped off the downhill side, and I went right behind him. Lord Jim just kept banging away with that Sharps Fifty.

Curly swung up on the front end of the caboose. I missed and had to hook on to the railing at the back end with my claw. Might not seem much to some two-fisted gents, but my right hand was full of my carbine. There was that, and then there was the fact that if I used my claw to hook on to something of substance, something with weight or pull to it, and I couldn't keep my elbow bent, that durn claw would come right off. See, it was tied by a thong above my elbow.

I locked that elbow and then clamped my carbine inside the railings on the stairs and turned it sideways. I was hooked on, though my feet was dragging and bouncing off the dang cross-ties.

I thought maybe my right shoulder would be pulled out of its socket, as I was at a peculiar angle. I wondered what else could go wrong, and right then the bandits mounted up and come pounding down the hill at us, and blazing away.

One bullet splintered the back door, another broke the glass, and a third pinged off the steel railings of the back deck and nicked my head.

Just then that corporal yanked open the door, laid the shotgun on the platform, and grabbed me like a rag doll and snatched me up. I dropped my carbine, but it didn't fall off as he dragged me half inside. A couple of the bandits was closing in on us, and durned if Squeak weren't one of them.

Curly stepped over my legs onto the platform and picked up that ten gauge.

"Try this!" he yelled and let go at them. Between his legs, I saw Squeak and one other bandit knocked out of their saddles. The last bandit swung away, back uphill.

The fight was over then, and we chugged off down the valley.

"You think you killed him?" I asked, as Curly pulled me to my feet.

Curly shrugged. "Squeak? Maybe not, but I put enough number four pellets in him that his skin won't make nobody a good pouch any time soon."

We left the corporal in the caboose, and me and Curly went topside and worked our way slow forward to the passenger car. I was pleased and surprised that nobody was hurt there.

Lord Jim said, "That was interesting. What now?"

We weren't but maybe thirty miles out of Woodward, about

halfway back to Canadian, so I thought Curly would want to stop the train, get off, and go run those bandits down.

I said, "Curly, we gonna go after them, right?"

He thought a minute, then shook his head.

"No, Brodie, we'll just press on."

"But Squeak got a good chunk of your money. Or his partners do, if you killed him."

"Thing is, Brodie, I got a lot more still on me. Mine and Billy's. Once we get Billy's money to him and Conchita, and the rest of mine back to my wife, maybe then. I'll put out some feelers afore we leave Canadian."

About then Wade walked in.

"It looked to me like we was picking up speed, 'stead of slowing down. I climbed back over the coal car and come through the baggage car, but if you think I need to stay up front, I'll go back. We ain't stopping to go after 'em?"

I said, "No, Son. Maybe later. Uncle Curly wants to get our stash of cash to where it can do some good. Anybody hurt up front?"

"No, no sir, Pop, not bad anyways. One bullet come by my head, bounced off the walls some, and hit the fireman in the ankle, but it weren't much. Big bruise, no blood."

He was strung up tight like he'd drunk a whole pot of coffee, hopping from one foot to the other, wiping his nose, and nodding his head. It wasn't until right then that it hit me that I had put my fifteen-year-old stepson in the middle of some serious danger, just bringing him along with me.

I muttered, "Sweet Jesus!"

He blinked a few times and said, "What is it, Pop? What's wrong?"

My mouth was too dry to answer. Curly stood and put his meaty hand on Wade's shoulder.

"Ain't nothing wrong, Wade. Your daddy just come to grips

with you being in your first gunfight. I believe it has brought him up short."

"But nothing's wrong. I ain't hurt. That's the most excitement I ever had. I'm still about to piss down my leg a little. I might of even hit one of 'em."

I said, "No fooling?"

"Yessir. Yessir, I think so. He was furthest on the right. Red shirt. I led him a little, like shooting birds. He dropped his rifle and turned away uphill."

Lord Jim said, "I saw that, too. I was trying to line up on him when he bent over and spun away."

Curly said, "Good shooting, boy. I've seen grown men seize up first time they was shot at, unable to return fire or even spit."

I put my hand on the back of Wade's neck and squeezed it.

"You done good, Son. You make me proud. I don't know how much of this we can tell your momma, though. Not if you want to ride with me again. She's likely to ground-stake you, and kill me. Now quit dancing around and go pee out the back door."

I apologized to the teacher for my language, plopped down beside Lord Jim, and reached for the flask he held out to me. Curly grabbed it first, took a long pull, then passed it to me.

"Squeak, that back-stabbing little SOB—I hope I gave him a death wound. And I hope it comes to him slow."

I said, "Maybe you did."

He said, "I don't think so. Little booger is tough as nails. I just had him figured for more character."

I thought on that for a while. I finally said, "Curly, what makes a man change sides like that? Somebody as has been on the straight and narrow for so long?"

"I ain't sure, Brodie. Usually it's the young'uns, right off the mark. Excitement, danger, easy money, sure as can be they gonna live forever. One hard cattle drive and they say to hell with this, I'm taking a softer and easier path. They go for the plunder . . . cattle, horses, banks."

"Yeah, Curly, but most of 'em die young, too. I'm talking about somebody like that preacher who went bad, or one of these old lawmen who starts robbing stages. Look at Squeak. He was a dependable cow puncher for what, ten or fifteen years?"

"Maybe they can't see no end to it, Brodie. How do you build a nest egg on thirty to fifty dollars a month? I married good. You and Emmalee got a nice saloon alongside your pay as a lawman. Lord Jim there, he robs fools legal-like . . ."

"All the while watching for a comfortable widow," said Lord Jim. "I'm only thirty. I'm also looking for a gambling house, ripe for takeover."

Curly said, "Wanting a comfortable widow hisself is most likely what tipped Squeak over the edge. I think that boy felt like I stole my missus out from under his nose, back when her husband died. Squeak had worked for them for some time, and he made some sideways comments on that very point. Ain't I right, Brodie?"

I nodded. As usual, everything Curly said made sense. Not as if I'd argue, anyways.

"I don't know what I'm gonna do," said Wade. "Work for Pop, I guess."

Curly snorted. "You go to school is what you do. Get trained as a lawyer. More and more of a need for that. You'd have men like me knocking down your door, soon as you hung a shingle."

"Good advice," said Lord Jim. "Much as I hate them, they are necessary. And honest ones are rare."

Chapter Eight

We unloaded in Canadian and recovered my shotgun from the corporal, who was continuing south. I thanked him for yanking me aboard and told him to look me and Wade up if he was ever back in Mobeetie. He gave me a funny look. I didn't learn why until days later.

There was plenty of daylight left, and, since Tascosa was more than two days' ride, we decided to eat some jerky and head on out to the west.

We made it into Tascosa late on the third day after leaving Canadian. Ain't no way you can imagine the whooping and hollering that went on once Billy and Conchita spied Curly and me. It got louder once Curly handed over Billy's money and guns.

Old Kendall was the blacksmith as well as Conchita's stepdaddy, and he was dancing around shouting, "Hot damn! Hot damn!" His wife, Senora Terrazas, was Conchita's momma. She was doing that Mexican trilling thing that sounds sort of like a whistle and hugging and kissing Curly.

They was all admiring Wade, who must of grown about a foot since they'd seen him two years back, and of course they all wanted to hear how Emmalee was doing.

When things slowed down some, Kendall said, "I'll get the missus and Conchita to kill us a lamb and fix us up some stew. That sound all right?"

It sounded just fine to all except Lord Jim. "I have my tongue all set for some beef," he said. "If I don't offend anyone, I'll return to my favorite parlor for a steak and a card game. Perhaps I'll see you fellow travelers before you leave for Curly's ranch?"

"Bank on it, Your Majesty." Curly clapped him on the back.

"Heckfire, Abernathy, we liable to drop in for a drink after we eat. Some of us, anyways. I ain't got enough likker here for barely one pass." Kendall paused and looked around for support, then went on. "I'm right sure we will."

Kendall was right. We ate and then headed over to Jenkins Saloon and found Lord Jim at a five-man table, in front of a mess of money. In fact, his shiny Colt was pinning down a right serious stack of paper money, but he looked worried.

"Good evening, gentlemen," he said as he stood. To the other players he said, "I fold. Deal me out of the next hand, please, as I must see what brings my friends."

He steered us away from the table, but I kind of hung back to watch his stash of winnings. None of them other players seemed too happy, nor too shy for theft. They was all staring at my hook and carbine, and if they was intimidated one bit they failed to show it.

Lord Jim was sort of whispering. "I have just had the damndest run of good luck I can remember. Those boys rode in from Colorado just last night, having had themselves a grand time at poker up there, and I have just relieved them of those winnings. I have delicately mentioned my very good friends, Deputy Billy, Marshal Sentell, and Marshal Dent, but they profess no knowledge of any of you."

Curly said, "So?"

"So, I need you to require my immediate presence elsewhere. A robbery, fire, whatever. We'll recover my profits and go over to the Equity Bar for a drink. On me, of course."

Billy was the most clear-headed amongst us, as he was the

deputy and didn't drink. He said, "They'll let you walk?"

"I believe that is a possibility."

Curly said, "And you don't think they'll follow us?"

Lord Jim shrugged and smiled. "There is that possibility as well." He glanced back at his poker companions. "Probably more than a possibility."

Kendall said, "Shit. All I wanted was another drink. Lemme go borry Jenkins's shotgun. Leastways in the street we ain't likely to hit so many innocents."

I said, "What innocents? Has y'all looked around?" I mean, this was the same tavern as kicked off the great Tascosa gunfight of 1886.

Kendall went to get the street howitzer that Jenkins kept behind the bar. Eighteen-inch ten gauge with a pistol grip.

Curly put a fist in Lord Jim's back and steered him back to the poker table.

"Hate to spoil your fun, boys, but I need Deputy Abernathy right now. He don't want to quit, but I ain't give him that option. We finish up our little problem, he'll be back. Pick up your poke, Abernathy."

Lord Jim started to scoop up his cash, but one of the losers grabbed his wrist.

"Hang on, there, pardner. Why not you just leave that 'til you come back?" The man stood and put his other hand on his revolver.

Curly tilted his big Winchester up until it was level with the cowpoke's crotch. Cocked it.

"You messing with my posse?"

I cocked my carbine. Wade cocked his. Kendall cocked both barrels of that ten gauge, behind the players. All those clicks seemed to have a soothing effect on them cowboys.

Curly said, "Y'all follow us into the street, y'all might be mistook for the men we're after."

They nodded slowly, and we eased out. Happy ending, or so it seemed. I should have known better. Tascosa never changed much, start to finish.

The Equity Saloon was laid out like a lot of others I been in. Off to the left was two tables, then the bar. It run the length of the rest of that wall. On the right was another table, then the billiards set-up, then two more poker tables in the rear.

Only thing sort of open was the table inside on the right. That might have saved us.

Lord Jim hustled off the two drunk bullwhackers at that table, got us seated, and then ordered beer. And something else.

"I summarily ruined those boys over in Jenkins's place," he said. "Best streak I've had in months. I hope you'll join me in some chilled oysters to celebrate. We'll do steaks later."

"I might could," I said.

"Do what?" growled Curly, his left eyebrow up to his hairline.

"Delightful raw shellfish," said Lord Jim. "Not unlike your clams, I think."

"Raw?" said Wade.

"You shitting me?" said Kendall.

"I had 'em once as a boy, over to the Texas coast," I said. "Look like a gob of spit, but they go down well if they's good and cold." I knew this wasn't going to play well but thought it would be fun to watch. I winked at Lord Jim and nodded for him to order them.

The food and beer came shortly before the unhappy card players from the other saloon. This is sort of how it happened.

Lord Jim pulled off his hat, a homburg or something like that, and knocked back two oysters. I tried one, too. It weren't fresh, I'll warrant, but it was edible. Surely wasn't no call for Wade's reaction when he tried one.

He gagged, grabbed his throat, and pushed out the front

door. The men he pushed by were the same ones Lord Jim had cleaned out at Jenkins's place, as they come in looking for us.

They come in sort of hard and fast, and I believe they was focused on the card tables in the back. Anyways, they blew right past us.

"Where's that card cheat of an Englishman?!" one of them shouted. It got right quiet for a Tascosa saloon just then. There they stood, four pissed-off cowpokes, hands on their gun butts. With their backs to us.

As you might guess, Curly figured it out first. He stood, drew both Schofields, and cocked them. Lord Jim was up and ready with his Colt a half second later. I was right behind him with my carbine, and Kendall, a sensible married man, dove under our table.

Those cowboys should have froze, hearing them guns cocked behind them. Trouble was, they was half in the tank and weren't none of them gunfighters no ways. They turned back and tried to draw.

Curly yelled, "Hold it!" And they did. I half took in a breath, thinking we'd missed a serious fight by an eyelash.

Might have, too, but then Wade staggered back in and said, "Was that them same cowboys that Lord Jim beat at cards?" I think ducking out and back into the light messed up his vision.

One of the cowboys said something rude, pulled his pistol, and Curly shot him. Two more drew or tried to. Lord Jim shot one, and I dropped the other. The fourth man backed away, hands up, then turned and ran right out the back door.

There was so much smoke I could hardly see beyond my gun barrel. Curly had to shoot the rude one again, and Lord Jim put two more rounds in his man. Mine stayed down.

Just another slow night in Tascosa. Made me right lonely for Mobeetie, which wasn't exactly some cowboy paradise itself.

Chapter Nine

"Those boys was Lazy S cowpunchers," Kendall said, as we walked back to his place. "Big spread, maybe twenty miles west. Must of just come back from pushing a herd north."

Wade said, "Lazy S?"

"Sideways *S*. Like if it was laying down. They got maybe fifteen riders."

"Maybe twelve now," said Curly. "Did that last one head home?"

"He did," said Kendall. "I checked. Straight for the ranch. They ain't no road, though. Kind of rough country, 'specially with it full dark. He'll play hell getting there before dawn."

Curly scrunched up those bushy eyebrows. "What do I think? I think we load up and head for my place. Right now. Billy and Conchita, too. They can stay with me and the missus long as they please, and welcome, too. I got work for 'em."

Lord Jim said, "I suppose I should go elsewhere also. Mobeetie, perhaps. I know the law there." He winked at Wade. "And there are several gambling establishments."

"Here's the thing, though," Kendall said. "I was gonna tell you later. They's closing Fort Elliot. Ain't gonna be nobody much in Mobeetie for long."

I said, "It'll fold like a tent. Judas Priest. That's how come that soldier give me that funny look."

Curly stopped, pulled off his hat, and scratched his bald noggin. "Here's what we'll do," he said. "Me and Billy and Conchita will take Lord Jim and ride for my place. Brodie, you and Wade go pick up Emmalee from Mobeetie, and y'all come on down, too. Pronto."

I said, "We might as well. Won't be no future there for lawmen nor saloon owners."

Wade said, "Good. I miss Momma Em, and ain't no young girls in Mobeetie anyways. None that ain't working, at least."

Curly said, "Let's get at it. Kendall, you might be safe here, but you and your missus is welcome, too."

"She might want to be near her baby. Her and Billy liable to make one them own selves anytime now. I'll ask her. Do she say yes, can I bring my wagon, anvils, and such?"

The next hour was the closest thing to a tornado that Tascosa had seen for a while. You never witnessed such a scramble. Wade and me was ready first but hung back to help Kendall load his wagon. Miz Terazzas made some deal with another Mex sheepherder on Kendall's animals, and we lit out, us to the east and them southeast. Wasn't yet midnight.

As we rode toward Mobeetie, Wade said, "Did Uncle Curly and Lord Jim need to shoot those men again, once they was down?"

I said, "Well, they must of felt it was necessary."

He wouldn't let it go. "You didn't."

"My man weren't breathing, Son. Listen now. If you are shooting with a man, or men, you remember this: as long as they can move they can kill you. And if they don't die they can come again for you later. You want to look over your shoulder the rest of your life?"

"Well, no, but . . ."

"Well, nothing. Uncle Curly don't want to, for durn sure. Me neither."

"So, y'all just don't take prisoners."

I said, "Not so much, not once the shooting starts. I got no interest in being backshot by some rowdy I winged and arrested some time in the past. And nor do I wish to meet with one in court on some trumped-up charges with a bought-out judge or jury."

Wade just grunted.

I said, "You heard Curly tell 'em to hold it. Both of us has almost always offered villains a way out. Way I see it, three of 'em chose to die tonight. Other one didn't."

Wade said, "So he ran off. Like we're doing, now."

I said, "That's right."

"Another thing," he said, "I think those three y'all shot was drunk."

"I don't doubt they was all four drunk. What, you figure we shoulda gone light on them? Maybe waited for the one that run to round up ten more punchers, get 'em likkered up, and come after us?"

"Well, no, Pop, but—"

"That's what it sounds like. Try and learn this, Son. Likker and pride kills more men than spotted fever. Now think on that and stop talking. You have very nearly pissed me off."

The ride from Mobeetie to Curly's ranch seemed right serene, given the past ten days. Curly's missus took us in like we were her own, and then Curly set about giving everybody jobs. He didn't have a problem with anyone but me. Lord Jim had rode on towards Wichita Falls.

"Brodie," he said, "you ain't fit for nothing but the law."

Miz Sentell steered me and Emmalee to a comfortable looking room and said it was ours, long as we chose to stay. Curly followed us in.

"Don't get too snug, Brodie. Come dawn, you and me is going to the Ranger camp up on the Red. Put you back on a payroll. Better get you some sleep soon as we eat."

The trail we were following cut an angle across the rocky side of this mountain we were on. Had to be pretty high up, as there wasn't anything growing there. I don't remember it being cold or windy, but it sure seemed like it ought to be.

I still can't tell you anything much about the gaggle of folks I was leading. Some women and children is all I can bring to mind, but no names. And how I came to be in charge was beyond me.

When we got to the top, it turned out to be the lip of a crater, maybe half a mile across. It was a kind of funnel, like a upside-down Chinee straw hat. Pretty bare, but at the bottom was a spring, and there were some bushes around the pool. Might have been inviting, but there was this pack of big, old, gray wolves that was milling about the water.

Soon as they saw us, two things happened. First off, the wolves started snarling and pacing back and forth, staring uphill at us. Next was that one of the children, didn't look big enough to walk, he squealed and took off downhill, right at them hairy monsters.

The rest of us froze. Nobody had a gun. Heckfire, I didn't even have a knife. My heart climbed up in my throat, and then I started running after the kid. Halfway down it come to me that there weren't any way out of this for me. It weren't like I had a choice, and it weren't even my boy.

There weren't even any rocks to pick up and throw. I thought, maybe I can scare them enough so's the boy can get away. I flung out my arms and tried to scream and roar like a bear, but what came out sounded like I was choking or gargling sand or something. My last thought before I piled into the wolves was maybe somebody will write something nice about me. That's about when Emmalee slapped me.

"Brodie! Brodie! Wake up!" she yelled. "You old fool, you sound like you're choking."

I quit thrashing pretty quick and said, "I was trying to yell to scare off some wolves."

"Wolves?"

"Uh-huh, wolves, Em. Down in some crater. They was about to eat this little boy. And me."

"Nightmare," she said. "Pretty good one, too, from the sounds of it. You liked to have scared me to death flailing about and gagging and all. Good thing you weren't wearing your hook or you might have put out my eye. Or yours. Why didn't you just shoot the durn wolves?"

"I didn't have a gun on me. Nobody did."

She snorted. "Fat chance of that. Sounds more like a fairytale than a bad dream."

I was still right agitated. "I felt so helpless, Emmalee. What do you think it means? Is it a premonishitive, you reckon?"

"Premonition? Lord, Brodie, now you've got me full awake. No, I doubt it's a premonition. More likely it's a reminder to stay out of craters full of wolves unless you're well-armed. You want some pie?"

The pie helped, but I got to tell you something. I been up against men with guns more than once, been shot at and hit, but ain't nothing scared me like that dream. I set out right then to push it down and away from my mind, but I never could. Not for a right long time, anyhow.

Chapter Ten

Ribeye Johnson had a reputation as a dependable tracker in the marshals' service, long before he moved from Indian Territory to Texas. I was right happy to be working with him in his new job as a Texas Ranger. It was sort of a new job for me, too. See, while I had been a Ranger in my younger and more wholesome days, so to speak, I had only just rejoined the force once I gave up my job as city marshal of Mobeetie.

Which I only did because the job was done away with, once the U.S. Army shut down Fort Elliot.

And it weren't like the Rangers were fired up to get me back, what with me missing the best part of my left hand. It had took Curly Jack Sentell completely losing what little level temper he had with the Ranger commander. Curly offered a shoot-off between him and the head Ranger, as well as between me and all the other Rangers in the camp. With all of us being the targets.

Curly never was much for halfway measures.

Anyways, it worked. Turns out a lot of the old and some of the new Rangers had worked with me and Curly over the years, and they pushed the captain to hire me. Three even said they wouldn't go up against me.

This job interview took place in a Ranger field camp along the Red River, not far from Curly's LT ranch. The Ranger captain yelled out, "Cookie! Toss one of them empty boxes in the river, and let's see can this man hit it." To me he said, "And don't you be pulling out no shotgun."

The cook dumped some cans from a crate and slung it on out in the water.

I drew my belt pistol, a Smith and Wesson double-action Frontier, laid it on my left forearm, and put all five rounds through the crate. I looked at Curly, and he nodded, so I unshucked my Colt Lightning carbine, clipped my hook on the slide, and pumped eight more rounds of .44-40 into the crate fast, as it splintered and broke into pieces.

Somebody might have whistled, but nobody said much as I reloaded. Finally, Curly said, "And you ought to see him in a knife and claw fight."

When the laughing stopped, the captain said I was hired.

Curly had mounted up and said, "I ain't sure why we had to go through all that. It ain't like they ain't enough nefarious goings-on in west Texas that we needs to be picky about body parts on good men. You try and keep these new folks straight, Brodie. Me and the missus will look after Miz Emmalee in your absence."

He rode off a good ten yards before turning back. "And you see that little sumbitch Squeak, try and wing him and save him for me. I don't need to tell you that."

I grinned. "No, sir, you don't. Goes without saying."

He nodded and was gone, with never a thank you or by-your-leave to the hard-assed Ranger captain he had just pretty much forced to hire me. That was ten days back.

Now, though, me and Ribeye was on a scout for Mister Nefarious hisself, one Muley Lefevre. Muley was a wiry little cuss, likeable as you could ask for when he was sober, which he almost never was. Drunk, he was mean as a cottonmouth moccasin, which, unlike a rattler, won't give out no warning. Heckfire, as a boy I've had one drop off a limb into my boat and try to bite me. I'm pleased they ain't found here in West Texas.

Muley's most recent misstep was shooting a Mex-Mescalero boy who'd been unlucky enough to walk into that alley by the rail station in Amarillo where Muley had just shot and robbed a customs agent.

The revenue man lived, but the breed didn't. I don't know how hard we would of pressed after Muley if his only crime was a wounded tax collector, but killing the boy was a whole different thing. We knew a bunch of half-breeds, and most weren't half bad.

In fact, the first real witness we come upon was a breed, the dead boy's half brother, a Mex-darky. Seems they had grown up close, despite having different daddies. They had just finished a bucket of beer and stepped outside the saloon. Nieto, the dead boy, had stepped into the alley when two shots rang out, then one more. Jonesy, the surviving brother, ran into the alley to see Muley take money off the downed revenue man. Muley fired another shot at Jonesy, missed, and staggered out the back end of the alley. Jonesy had no gun, so he fled back out into the street, but not before noticing that his favorite half brother had been shot in the forehead.

Jonesy told me that he knew that was not a good thing. He said his brother's last words had been, "I got to go pee. I'll step in the alley," shortly before taking a bullet in the brain pan.

Things moved faster after that. Ribeye learned that Muley had stolen a mare that had come in for shoes, and the job was half done. Couldn't of been much easier to track.

Soon as we set out after that two-shoed, tenderfoot mare, I asked Ribeye about his name.

"You do know what a ribeye is, right?"

" 'Course I do. Cowboy steak. It's why I ask," I said.

"Well, see, my name is Reeby. R-double e-b-y. Sounds like *Reebee*, but spelt different. Reeby was my mother's brother. Naturally these old boys out here gonna call me Ribeye."

"Sort of pre-ordained."

That started our conversation as we rode straight south toward the community of Lubbock.

"I heard about you and that claw back while I's still up in the Indian Territory. Folks said you and old Sentell rode together some."

I said, "We did, off and on. Still do. He is who got me back in the Rangers."

Ribeye looked at me sideways and grinned. "What did you do to piss him off?"

I smiled back. "What, you ain't delighted to be trailing a murderous little drunk across miles and miles of flat plains? Sleeping on caliche rock? Hoping he ain't got a rifle?"

"Not exactly," he said. "It's why I asked."

"Well, pissing off Curly Jack Sentell is one thing I work special hard to avoid. You ever seen him worked up?"

"No, sir. Can't say as I have. I mean I ain't sure. I did know a Sentell, back in the war, but he weren't called Curly Jack. I have heard this one is firm but fair."

I laughed. "Firm ain't the word for it, if he ain't total happy. Fair? Yeah, right fair I guess, long as he likes you or don't see you as a threat."

"And if he does?"

"Then it's Annie Bar the Door. Curly ain't much on negotiating. He goes straight at a problem."

Ribeye shrugged and said, "Changing the subject some, you make out that thread of smoke, little off to the left?"

"I do. Pencil thin, going straight up. Ain't a drop of wind nowhere. Want to head that ways?"

"Yep," he said. "I might can just make out some trees there. Probably water. Muley will head there, too, most likely."

"Lord, Ribeye, you got good eyes. At least it ain't some house afire."

Turned out the smoke was from some greasy mesquite wood, heating bath water for a road house in Plainview. Plainview was a crossroads town of maybe seven low buildings, and about the same number of people. Muley had been through there a few days before.

The old Mexican who ran the roadhouse said, "He was here. He took my good mule, left me a crippled horse. Tried to take my daughter, too."

"Headed for Lubbock, was he?"

"*Si,* Señor. That's where he goes."

"You ever seen a wiry little Texan, high voice? Name of Squeak?" I known it was a long shot, but there were gracious few people to ask anything, out on those plains.

"*Si,* he was here, too. I dunno, maybe six days ago? With three other hombres. Trouble, I think. They go east."

Ribeye said, "How come you figured them for trouble?"

The old man thought a moment, then said, "They been shot. Two, anyhow. They wash themselves up here, I see the wounds. Not so old, them bullet holes."

"And where'd they come from?"

"East. They come from east, rest here some, go back east. And they tried to get the thief you are chasing to go with them. But he say he got business in Lubbock."

I'd have to wire that fact to Curly, soon as we got to Lubbock. Didn't make sense, less Squeak was looking for revenge, and that would be insane. Revenge on Curly Jack? Pure insane.

We got lucky in Lubbock. Muley Lefevre was sleeping it off in the jail. He had took on a load of demon rum and mouthed off at a "damn Mexican" who turned out to be a deputy sheriff.

Ribeye took care of the paperwork for us to transport Muley back to Amarillo, soon as he sobered up. I went to the telegraph office and sent a wire to the Ranger camp and asked them to relay the news about Squeak to Curly.

As we got ready to pick up Muley from the jail, a wire come in from Curly, saying head straight back to the LT Ranch once we deposited Muley's sorry butt in the Amarillo jail. Didn't say why, but we figured it had to do with Squeak.

Wrong again.

Chapter Eleven

Turns out Squeak was keeping a low profile, leastways anywhere near Curly Jack Sentell. I remember thinking that maybe Squeak was smarter than I give him credit for.

No, what I'd been summoned for was that Curly's old commander from back in the war had visited the ranch, and it weren't by chance. Governor Sul Ross had come to see Curly to invite him and his missus to join him in College Station when he went to take over the college there.

I scratched my head. "Never heard of no College Station. Where's it at?"

Curly said, "Northeast of Austin and northwest of Houston, over there in the Brazos Valley. They call it Texas AMC, which stands for Agriculture and Mechanic College, I think he said. I didn't know of it either, exactly."

"Why's he expect y'all to come?"

We were sitting in rockers on the wide porch around Curly's hacienda; both our ladies were there, too. Curly stood, walked to the edge, and poured out the dregs of his coffee. He lit a cigar and stared off to the east. Toward this College Station place, I reckon.

"Hell, Brodie, I ain't sure. He was my general in the war; he's the durn governor now, and fixing to be president of this college. He can expect whosoever he pleases to come, and, if they know him, they'll be there."

"How come?"

"You really don't know squat, do you? Sullivan Ross fought the Comanche as a Ranger before the war. Took a fifty-eight-caliber ball in the chest and near died. When the war come, he commanded the Sixth Texas Cavalry early on, then took in the Ninth and Twenty-Seventh Texas Cavalry regiments, as well as mine."

"You was in the Third Texas, right?"

"I was, Brodie, and it's right nice to see you ain't forgot every last thing I told you. Any ways, we was then called Ross's Cavalry Brigade. When the war ended, Ross was only twenty-six years old. Must have been in a hundred fights, and every man who served with him would've charged a two-gun battery with a pitchfork if General Ross said to."

"But you was only a captain, right? So how'd you come to be on the general's invite list?"

"Right at the end we were covering Hood's retreat out of Nashville. Ross happened to be in my company's part of the line when we got hard pressed. It was intense and a near thing, but we turned 'em back. Him and me got to know each other there in that fight, and during the long pullback that followed."

I stood and stretched. "Well, I enjoyed the history lesson, but I guess I'd better get on over to the camp. The captain is liable to be right upset with me already for stopping by and spending the night with Emmalee."

"Your captain is already took care of, Brodie. I didn't call you here to try and learn you something. What it is, is that you and Emmalee and Wade is going with me and the missus and Billy to College Station this week."

"Us? And Billy?"

"Yessir, and Conchita."

"What the hell, Curly?"

"Billy's going in that mechanic's school. General Ross done said so. Conchita's gonna help set up and run the Ross household at the college. You and Wade and me is gun cover, since Squeak's still out there somewheres. Emmalee and my missus is along to contradict us and try and keep us off the crooked path, there and back."

I looked over to Emmalee, who was sitting in the porch swing with Mrs. Sentell. Big smiles all over both faces.

"So, Miz Emmalee Dent, you knew about this last night and didn't let on?"

"Curly wanted to explain it to you, and last night I was sort of busy."

I choked a little, and Mrs. Sentell said, "You did rush through supper, Mister Dent."

Emmalee said, "Brodie, you are blushing." She was blushing a little herself.

Curly said, "Main problem has been keeping Billy and Conchita and Wade quiet. They has all near wet themselves, wanting to tell you."

Somebody signaled them right then, and they came busting out the front door. Conchita hugged everybody, and Billy pumped my hand and Curly's and thanked us both. Wade just stood there beaming.

I said, "No need to thank me, Billy. I didn't have a durn thing to do with this."

The thing was that I couldn't find a thing wrong with the plan. Even looked like it might be kind of fun, but nobody had asked me anything about it. I was just told what would happen, and that brought me right low. Like I didn't matter. On top of it, I felt kind of petty for feeling that way.

Billy said, "Uncle Curly told your captain, and he said go ahead on. Said they wouldn't need you."

And I thought I couldn't feel worse. Anyhow, I took a deep breath and said, "Curly, I need you to hang on and back up some. I get that you and this general or governor or whatever he is, y'all are close, and he wants you and Miz Sentell to be there when he's sworn in. What I don't get is how me and Emmalee and the young'uns got put in the mix."

Curly snorted and huffed and jabbed a finger at me. "Try and pay attention this time. I'm invited because Sul Ross thinks I saved his life. Miz Sentell is going because she's my wife. Emmalee is going because my wife says so, and you don't never do nothing nice for her. You're going 'cause Emmalee says so; Billy's going 'cause I asked the governor about what this school is for, and, when he told me about the mechanic's and machinery part of it, I told him all about Billy and his spare parts business. You know, for people. Sul Ross called Billy in and talked to him some, and then he said Billy was exactly the kind of student they was looking for. Said there was a way it wouldn't cost Billy nothing."

"Scholarship program," Emmalee said.

"That's what he called it. Said he had some leeway on who got one of the, ah, those . . ."

"Scholarships," said Emmalee.

"Right," Curly said. "Thank you, Em. Anyways, he said he could give Billy one, what with him being the new president and all."

I said, "No cost. Good Lord. What about Conchita?"

Curly smiled. "Billy said he wouldn't go without her. Sul Ross said that was fine, as he was gonna have to find himself a housekeeper anyways. Any of this getting through to you?"

I said, "I think I got that much. How you plan to get there?"

"I bought me a mud wagon cheap when one of them little stage lines went under. It's got a top and good side canvas. We'll tote the women and baggage in it to Wichita Falls. Take trains from there." He paused. "I'll stash that wagon at the rail head for the return trip, and we can see if Lord Jim's still hanging around there."

"What you need with him?"

"Well, Brodie, since you Rangers ain't been able to snare Squeak or even spot him, I thought we'd ask what Lord Jim has heard."

"What if he's got a line on Squeak?"

"I'll send your butt after him, Ranger Dent, whilst I see the women and young'uns safely to College Station."

We left early the next morning.

The ride to Wichita Falls went smooth with Billy and Wade handling the wagon, and me and Curly Jack ranging ahead some. That way we could show Billy the way, watch for trouble, and mainly stay in front of all the dust that wagon kicked up.

We made Wichita Falls before dark. Curly said, "Me and the boys will drop the women and baggage at that hotel right there, then go by the livery."

"And me?"

"I want you to see can you find Lord Jim. Bring him to the hotel bar. But you know what? Best you check on the train schedule first. We're looking to go through Fort Worth to Waco for starts."

I nodded and wheeled my horse around, before he come up with more tasks. I did manage to throw Emmalee a kiss as I rode past the wagon.

The station master was scrawny, bald, bespectacled, and ill-tempered, like most of them I ever met. I think maybe it was a job requirement.

"Southbound?" he said. "Well, sir, they is a train due here somewhere around nine tomorrow. Y'all should have no problem getting on it. Horses, too, if you can pay."

I grinned and said, "You do mean nine A.M., right?"

He said, "I do, but it could be P.M. Listen for it, or just ride on."

"You got any idea where a sporting man name of Lord Jim might be?"

"Try the Carriage House, other side of the livery from here. If he ain't there it ain't my fault. This ain't no information booth."

Lord Jim was there.

Chapter Twelve

I walked in the Carriage House Saloon, just after dark. It took a moment for my eyes to adjust, and Lord Jim spotted me first.

He was seated facing the door, of course, but stood and waved. "Marshal Dent! A sight for sore eyes, I declare. Do join us. Barkeep, another glass, please."

Wasn't much of a crowd, being more like suppertime. I scanned the place as I made my way to his table and heard him add in a lower voice, "Gentlemen, this game must be postponed. This is my good friend Brodie Dent, marshal of Mobeetie. Perhaps you've heard of him. Please excuse us."

The four poker players with him muttered and mumbled as they gathered their cash, until one actually looked back at me.

"Jesus," he said as he elbowed his neighbor. "The claw. It's him."

The others eased away except for one really big man, who just stood and stared at my star.

"Sure," he said with a heavy Irish accent, "and would that be a Ranger badge?"

"It would be. Fort Elliot folded, and the marshal's job folded with it. After many years, I'm back in the Rangers. Who's asking?"

He was huge, over six feet tall and the far side of two hundred-fifty pounds. Probably closer to three hundred. I eased my hand onto my pistol grip.

He smiled, and it lit up the room. Thanks be to God, he

stuck out a hand the size of a small town. "Pug O'Hanley. Maybe we could talk later."

Lord Jim pushed over to us. "Forgive me for being slow with the introductions. So, you're a Ranger. This is so fortuitous! Pug and I both being expatriates from the British Isles, we were just deliberating on his odds of becoming a Ranger himself."

My good hand was swallowed in O'Hanley's grip. I should have extended the claw. I said so. He apologized, released me, and turned to leave.

"No, Pug, not you. You stay. We'll pursue this Ranger business, as soon as we learn why Ranger Dent is here. I take it you're on business, Brodie?"

"Sort of. Curly Jack invited us to go to College Station to see the new college president get installed. By the governor, Sul Ross. Who's also the new president of A and M."

When they both looked stupefied, I added, "Agriculture and Mechanic's College. A and M."

They nodded slowly, so I barged ahead. "And they want Billy in the school. The mechanics part, that is. He's with us."

"Here? Billy's here? What about Conchita?"

"Her, too, Jim. She's gonna be the housekeeper for Sul Ross. Emmalee, Wade, and Miz Sentell are going with us, too."

"My God! Let's go see them. You, too, Pug."

I said "Good idea. Curly wants to know what you've heard from Squeak."

"I have spoken with him," Lord Jim said, in a kind of funny voice. We were walking as we talked.

I didn't like the sound of that. "You better just save that tale for Curly Jack. Squeak ain't still here, is he?"

"He is not, to my certain knowledge. Another Ranger showed up yesterday and said he was looking for Squeak and his bandit gang. O'Hanley and myself accompanied the Ranger to confront the bandits, but they learned of the Ranger and fled north. Followed by the Ranger, of course."

"You get the Ranger's name?"

"In fact, I did, Brodie. A Mister Johnson. Ribeye Johnson. Another of your colorful colonial names. I believe you know him."

"I surely do. Heckfire, we was on a mission together all last week."

"He said as much. Well, here's the hotel. Shall we go in?"

I said, "I think not. What I think is that Curly Jack will want to hear what you got to say before we get all tangled with introductions and catching up and all. Y'all wait here."

Minutes later I was back with Curly Jack. The four of us bunched up at one end of the hotel porch.

Curly shook hands and started right in. "Brodie says you been talking with Squeak?"

Lord Jim said, "Two days ago he came here and caught me alone coming out of my room. He braced me. He had two men with him with shotguns. I thought discretion the better part of bravado, so I acted glad to see him."

"Really?"

"Indeed. I said that you and I had a falling out over your wife and that as soon as I could put together a gang I wanted to raid your ranch. To kill you and make off with your money and your wife."

Curly said, "I expect he warmed to that idea. So, you strung him along so's you could get word to me?"

"That, or simply kill him. O'Hanley here and I were planning an ambush when Ranger Johnson arrived and scared the bandits away. In fact, the two of us were leaving to kill them when we learned of their rushed departure."

I said, "Curly, if anybody can trail them, it's Ribeye Johnson. He might be the best tracker in Texas."

"Yeah, Brodie, but can he handle all three of them once he

finds them? I might best send you to catch up and give him a hand."

"I doubt I'll get there in time to help him. I'm telling you, he's like a rat terrier."

At that moment, a lone rider appeared out of the dark and tied off at the rail not six feet from us. Light from the hotel window behind us probably blinded him.

"Has y'all seen Lord Jim Abernathy?"

It was Ribeye. Alone. Didn't have no dead banditos tied across no horses.

"Ribeye Johnson," I said. "It's good to see you again, I think. You all shot up?"

He dismounted. "No, sir. Not even shot at. I take it you done talked with Lord Jim?"

"He's right here with me, and I have just talked with him. Said as how you was hot on Squeak's trail, but here you are. Not even shot at. Your words, not mine."

Curly Jack snorted. "Rat terrier, Brodie? Your words, not mine. Well, I'm going back inside for a drink. Y'all can join me, or just stand around here talking about what you ain't done so far."

Inside, Curly Jack left Lord Jim to visit with the women and youngsters while the rest of us took a drink in the bar.

I took my first sip and said, "Well, Ribeye, where did you lose them? Could they be heading back here?"

"They picked up the trail of a small horse herd northeast of here and crossed the Red River with 'em. I lost their tracks in that mess. I ain't ashamed none. It will take more'n one man to pick up where they peel away from that lash-up." He stared at Curly.

Curly Jack stared back, for a moment. "I know you, don't I? Wasn't you with me when we caught them infiltrators one night in the war? But you wasn't called Ribeye. And you was wounded and sent off a few nights later."

"That was me. Time I could walk again, y'all had surrendered. My actual name is Reeby. And you wasn't called Curly Jack, neither."

Curly just snorted. "Maybe if you hadn't got hit, we could of fought on. Well, Ranger Johnson, Brodie says you're good. I'm gonna send him with you in the morning to see can you lock in on 'em again. And take this Pug feller, too, if he ain't too busy. I hear he wants to be a Ranger." He stared at the big man.

O'Hanley grinned. "Oh, and I'm available. However, there is the wee matter of pay."

"You'll draw Ranger pay. Same as these two, only out of my pocket. Pull your weight, and I'll see you signed up once you're back. You gonna need an advance?"

"No, sir. I don't believe in such. I'll take my pay once I've done the work, and I thank you for the lovely opportunity. I truly do. I will take another cup of kindness, if you like."

Sentell signaled for a bottle, then turned back to O'Hanley. "I know another O'Hanley, Mike O'Hanley, up to Canadian. Has a little school there. Skinny, compared to you. Is he family?"

O'Hanley brightened. "Michael O'Hanley is me dear cousin. Last I heard he was a priest up in Boston. Could it be himself?"

"It's him," Curly Jack said. "Used to wear the cloth. Come from Boston by way of Fort Lincoln and Deadwood, back in '76. Now, tell me about you. How come you want to ranger?"

"I ain't been but two things since I left Ireland, and that's a prize fighter and a lawman. I was a Mounty until I killed another Mounted Policeman with my fists. Fair fight, but I figgered it best to leave. Come south to Arkansas, I did, and was a deputy town marshal there for a good while. Nice country. Green, like home. I liked it." He looked off into nowhere.

Curly said, "So?"

O'Hanley shrugged. "So, I tracked some murderous pig thieves into the territory, where I had no jurisdiction. Killed them and left them for the wild hogs."

I said, "You killed them over some stolen pigs?"

"Not exactly. See, they had killed my boss. With an axe, over in Arkansas. Left his body for their pigs to feed on. I just returned the favor."

Everyone stared at him for a moment.

I said, "Jumping Jehoshaphat Christmas."

Curly Jack said, "I think I'm gonna like this boy. What we'll do is leave Lord Jim here in case Squeak doubles back, and y'all miss him somehow."

Chapter Thirteen

Me and Ribeye and Pug was ready, early next morning. Saddled, provisioned, pack mule all set by half past seven, but I wanted to see the other travelers safe on the train. Which, of course, was late.

When it finally started chuffing and them wheels begun spinning and screeching it was close to noon. Curly yelled out, "Don't kill him less you have to!" and they chugged away.

Lord Jim said, "I'll be alert for your man Squeak and do my best to delay him if he comes back before you. Should the opportunity present itself, though, I'll simply shoot him."

I swung into the saddle and said, "Try to wound him, in that case. You know, save him for Curly Jack."

He gave me a strange look. "I'm not very good at that wounding business."

I bent down close. "Curly really wants Squeak alive, Jim. You ain't got some reason to silence him, have you?"

He said, "Of course not. I'm just not that fine a marksman."

"Well, if you can't wound him, don't shoot him."

"Of course. I do see. I understand. Be safe now, and good luck. You will probably catch him anyhow."

Ribeye led us straight to that crossing on the Red River where the horse herd had passed over, followed by our banditos. We splashed across well before dark.

"We'd best split up here," Ribeye said. "Work both sides of

the mess them horse herders left. Ain't no telling which way these boys will go, and they just might trail this herd for a mite. Y'all work the right side."

We did. Trailed them until dark, with no sign of them splitting away.

Come dawn we were after them again, but Ribeye put Pug on the left side and kept me on the right. He went right up the middle.

I said, "I can see how come you couldn't track these boys alone. You trying to spot their trail following on top of the herd?"

He said, "I think I done spotted it. They's three horses riding together, right on top of them unshod ponies. I think what we got here is some Injin horses being drove up to Fort Sill, for sale to the U.S. Army."

Pug said, "What if our lads is scheming to take the herd and sell it them own selves?"

I got a chill down my spine.

"You done give me a chill, Pug. Let's go a little faster."

Not even two miles on we found the horse wranglers. Two Tonk boys, one young Mex, and one old one. All dead as the cold campfire they was laying around.

I said, "It appears our boy Squeak and his gang has graduated from robbery to murder and rustling horses."

Ribeye said, "It do. It surely do."

Pug dismounted and said, "Bloody bastards. Two of these boys look to be back shot."

Ribeye and me swung down, too.

"Well, we can't just leave 'em, but we can put 'em in one grave. Grab the pick and shovel, and we'll take turns."

Ribeye said, "We'll get the hole, Boss. Why don't you search 'em, see is they got anything will tell us who to notify."

"I'll do that," I said, "but I can swing a pick."

The old Mex had wore a cavalry hat that had the name tag

"A. Chavez" stitched inside. I tossed the hat to Ribeye.

"Could be him," I said. "Cut it out and hang on to it. We'll put his name on the wire soon as we come on a telegraph." I grabbed the pick.

The ground was soft. Two hours later we pushed on north.

"We'll push harder," I said. "The herd is easy to track, and them boys ain't about to abandon it."

Ribeye said, "I'd call them ponies 'walking dollar bills.' Them bandits is making straight for Fort Sill, all right. If any of them knows that area, they'll push the herd into some woods along Cache Creek. Hide out there 'til they make a sale."

"And where's this Cache Creek?"

"This here stream we been following. That's Mount Scott straight ahead. Fort is this side of it. They's a little shanty town, this side of the fort. We should go slow here on in. Watch them trees for horses."

"Me and Ribeye both favor the forty-four Winchester cartridge. All our revolvers and carbines is in that caliber," I said to Pug as we rode slowly alongside the creek. "I notice you don't. Ain't that carbine a single shot?"

"Faith, and it is," he said. "Had it since the Mounted Police first issued it to me. And I like the Schofield as my sidearm. Good cartridge, fast reloads."

Ribeye said, "Your carbine looks like an Enfield. I carried one during the war, before I took a Spencer off a Yankee."

"It's an Enfield, true enough, but one that has been through the Snyder conversion." Pug unsheathed it to show us. "Breech-loader."

He rolled open the breech and extracted the cartridge. It was the biggest bullet I'd ever seen.

"Judas Priest," I said. "Looks like a silver-tipped copper cigar. What size is that? Bigger than a Sharps Fifty, I'll warrant."

"Five seventy-seven Snyder," he said, tossing it to me. "I believe you colonials would call it a fifty-eight caliber. I'm not so much of a sharpshooter, am I, so's I need whatever I hit to stay down."

I studied it a minute and then tossed it to Ribeye. He weighed it, then passed it back to Pug and said, "You even point that cannon at me and I'd stay down."

We rode a ways on, and then I said, "Back up a minute, Ribeye. You was in the Confederacy? Same as old Curly Jack? You don't look to be that old."

Ribeye looked pained. "Well, I ain't too old, neither. I was twenty when the war ended, and I ain't but forty-seven now."

"Lord," I said. "You are about ten years older'n me. I figgered us to be about the same age."

"Well," Pug said, "ain't we a bunch of old farts. I'm near forty meself."

Chapter Fourteen

Such was the gossip and nonsense we passed back and forth as we made our way north slow. Anybody heard us might of thought we was three old women, rocking on the side porch. Then again, maybe not.

"I was with Sentell in the war, but he weren't no Curly Jack then," said Ribeye. "Sentell was called Cane Pole Jack back then. Y'all will no doubt wonder why."

I shook my head. "No doubt at all."

"Pray tell," said Pug. "I am near wet with anticipation."

Ribeye said, "Say what?"

Pug laughed. "I'm about to piss down my leg with curiosity is what."

Ribeye gave him a sideways look, then said, "I was there. It was late sixty-four or early sixty-five, I disremember, but anyways Sentell was our company commander, and it was real dark, and here come this here General Ross."

I said, "Same one as Curly has gone to see at that college?"

"The very same, and he tells Sentell to expect a Yankee attack right at dark. Problem was that we was stuck out on a point on a wooded ridge and didn't nobody know which side the Yanks would hit. Could be they'd come at us both ways."

Pug said, "Y'all couldn't cover both ways?"

"We was so short-handed by then, we could barely cover one side." Ribeye took a breath. "Just then we stopped two men sneaking up the ridge into our lines. They was wearing butternut jackets and said they's lost. Said they was from the Third Texas."

"Same as you and Curly," I said.

"Once again, the very same. Sentell says, 'What company y'all in?' and they says, 'Company B.' Sentell pointed his shotgun at 'em and says, 'Welcome home, boys, but I don't seem to remember you. This here is 'B' Company. My company.' He had them peel off them jackets and go face down on the ground. See, they was Yankees, trying to get a fix on our position."

I winked at Pug. "No fooling?"

"God's truth," said Ribeye. "Sentell ast them which side they was gonna hit, but they wouldn't say. One of 'em was a scared private, but the other was a crusty old hard-ass, probably a sergeant. I think the private was more scared of his sergeant than us, to begin with."

I said, "I guess Curly relieved him of that notion."

"That's exactly what happened. General Ross says, 'We got to know their plans right now,' and Sentell says back, 'I'm fixing to learn that, but it might be better that you not watch.' That general's eyebrows went right straight up."

Pug said, "He talked like that to a general?"

"I'm here to tell you, that's exactly what he said. Then he had me cut him a five-foot-long section of a cane pole maybe two inches across. Sentell handed me his shotgun and says, 'Spread their feet apart, and, if they tries to rise, put a load of buckshot in their crotch.' So I did."

I said, "Did what? Shot 'em?"

"Naw," he said. "I kicked their feet apart. Then Sentell says to the old one, 'I'm gonna whack you twenty times with this here stout cane. You decide you want to talk before I'm through, just sing out.' Then he rose up on his toes and hit that old Yank right across the small of his back, and said, 'One!'

"I think it hurt that old boy so bad he couldn't yell. He arched his back and turned sideways just as Sentell said, 'Two' and hit him again. Busted his left arm, and then number three broke a rib or two, so he rolled on his back. The old man said, 'Sweet Jesus!' And then the fourth lick caught the prisoner across the belly and doubled him up."

Pug said, "Sure, and I'm shocked the prisoner could even say a word."

"Naw, that was the general," said Ribeye. "I don't think the old sergeant could talk by then neither. I thought maybe that was Sentell's plan. Didn't nobody think that tough old bird was gonna sing, but his young partner in crime was laying there on his stomach, three feet away. Getting splattered with blood, hearing the sergeant grunt and groan. Through twenty whacks."

"What next?" I guess I could see it coming, but I had to ask.

"That boy's eyes was plumb bugging out of his skull. 'Your turn, youngster,' says Sentell, 'unless you're ready to help us out here.' The boy had done wet hisself, but he said, 'I can't.' He nodded at the bloody sergeant. 'He'll kill me, do I talk.' Sentell said, 'Your choice, then. One!' and stroked him hard across the back of his legs."

I said, "I bet he didn't last the full twenty."

"It only took the one lick. The boy flipped over and said, 'Don't hit me no more.' Tole 'em whatever they ast. Sort of slow at first, but then the old Yankee sergeant leaned over and spit in the young one's face."

Pug said, "Lord, love a duck. You don't exaggerate? Just a wee bit, maybe?"

"I swear it is the gospel truth. Then Sentell handed me that big stick and said, 'Johnson, whack that old boy about ten more times, slow-like, whilst I try to listen to this man.' Every time I hit the old sergeant, the youngster talked louder and faster."

Pug said, "I can't get over that old one. He had some tough

bark on him, didn't he?"

Ribeye said, "He purely did. If I hadn't seen it myself, I wouldn't repeat it. Anyways, when they come at us that night, we were total ready. We had a few Spencers, and 'A' Company had Colt repeating carbines. We lit them Yankees up. Blistered them, left a bunch kicking and screaming, and then we slipped away to another ridgeline farther south before dawn."

"Sure explains why Ross thinks so highly of Curly Jack," I said, "or, leastways, of Cane Pole Jack."

"Yessir," said Ribeye. "They'd have broke our whole line, had they got by us that night. That general told Sentell he woulda made him a colonel on the spot, 'cept that we already had a colonel. Sharp-dressed asshole name of Lew Turner, who wasn't nowhere to be found if there was fighting about."

I said, "I met him. He'd married a rich widder, took over her ranch, then he died, and Curly married his widder. She's a durn good woman, too. She was back there in Wichita Falls with Curly. Y'all met her by the train."

Ribeye said, "What happened to him after the war? I mean, was he a lawman on up to his marriage?"

"Sort of, kind of off and on. But Unionists was running Texas after the war and didn't want no ex-Confederates in the Rangers." I had to think a minute. "He was twenty when the war ended and was a shotgun rider on the Butterfield stages for a while, then rode with the Seventh Cavalry. Matter of fact, he was with 'em at the Washita River fight in late 1868. Being a Rebel captain was good enough to get him corporal stripes as a Yankee horse soldier. By 1870 he was out of the army and killing buffalos, when he weren't serving as a minuteman."

Pug said, "What are minutemen? I thought they went up against our fine redcoat boys, back in the last century."

I said, "He told me that the army nor the state house boys weren't doing anything to protect the frontier back then, so there was some volunteers in most counties who would saddle up and ride whenever there was an Indian raid. Or bandits, whatever. On a minute's notice. But, come 1871, he was in the Rangers and at the Keep Ranch fight, not too far from right here."

Ribeye said, "I heard of that one. Ten Rangers took on forty or so Comanche and Kioway?"

"That's what he told me," I said. "Best I remember, a couple of civilians was in it, too. Anyways, they all had Yellowboy Winchesters, and it must of been one of the first times they was used against the Redskins. Kindly took them by surprise."

"Talk about remembering?" Ribeye touched a finger to his head as it came back to him. "I just recalled something else on that night old Cane Pole got his name. As we laid there in the dark and waited for the Yanks, he says to us, 'Boys, check yor primers.' I ast him, 'How come you don't call 'em caps, like ever' one else?' He says, 'Was I to ast that, half these boys is so dumb, they would pull off their hats and study them.' We was nervous, I guess, but we all laughed so hard I near 'bout peed down my own leg. It took the edge off us, helped us be ready." Ribeye pulled up right then and said, "Hold on a bit. I seen movement ahead."

Before you could say, "Jack Rabbit," all three of us had our scopes out.

Chapter Fifteen

Ribeye said, "You see that smoke, do ye not? There's a small hut there. The movement is in them trees between the hut and the creek. Horses, I think."

I squinted and said, "I think you're right."

"I can't see nothing but the smoke," Pug said, "but the tracks is pointed right to it."

"We'll go up slow, single file," I said. "Stay in the trees, much as we can. Ribeye, you got the best eyes. You lead."

He frowned. "Me and my big mouth."

Two hundred yards closer we could all see the layout pretty good. Sod cabin, some sort of rail and wire fencing in the woods, with horses in a corral and pigs behind the wire. Wasn't much doubt in my mind those horses was the ones we was trailing. There was also a cook fire in the yard with two men turning some meat on a big spit.

"Cooking a pig, maybe?" Ribeye was sniffing. "I smell pork." He licked his lips.

"Did you just lick your lips? It's a pig," said Pug. "I hate pigs." He spat in the bushes. "There's also a body beside the hut."

Ribeye said, "You reckon they've commenced to fight amongst themselves?"

"Over a pig?" Pug spat again. "No, I'm leaning toward the body belonging to the owner of them porkers."

"Probably right," I said. "Means one of our banditos is either gone on to the fort or inside the soddy. Ribeye, you backtrack a ways, swing wide, and ride north. Maybe a half mile on, you ease back toward the trees, and work your way close on foot. Me and Pug will stash our horses here and get closer, too."

"What you want me to do when I'm up close?" Ribeye asked. "If I yell out they'll likely shoot me. Or leastways try."

"Just fire off a round once you're set," I said. "It'll startle the hell out of them, and we'll all move in on 'em then."

Pug said, "Faith, that's a fine plan. But I'd be a bit more comfortable if he were to stay close, but well hidden. In case their third partner shows up."

Ribeye nodded and slipped away.

Me and Pug tied off our mounts, pulled our long guns, and moved in, slow and easy. The plan was good, if I do say so myself, and it worked fine. Almost.

Forty yards from the pig farm we pulled up to wait for Ribeye to get in place and signal us. Pug was wheezing pretty good, but those pigs was milling about and snorting so much, wasn't nobody going to hear us. Then the pig stench hit us. Like a hammer.

Both of us choked some. We put down our carbines and pulled up our scarves over our noses, and Pug said, "Sweet Jesus," just a shade too loud.

Both bandits was sitting on stumps by the cook fire, and it was plain that Squeak weren't one of them. Anyways, Pug's comment had come in a sudden calm of pig snorting, and one of those bandits popped up and looked right at us and said, "Hey!"

We bent to retrieve our carbines just as he raised a shotgun toward us. Everything went slow then. I think I heard him cock it as I was standing up again, but suddenly his hat flew off at us, along with right much blood spray. He fell forward into the fire pit, just as we heard the bang of Ribeye's shot and saw his gunsmoke blossom from the bushes beyond the soddy.

The other bandit stood and faced toward Ribeye until Pug yelled, "On your belly, Boyo!"

We spread a little and moved in, but he turned toward us, pulled a large knife, then took off running toward the creek.

We ran, too, with me shouting, "Take him alive!"

He beat us to the creek bank, then turned on us. "I can't swim a lick!" he yelled at us.

I was puffing a bit, but Pug was breathing so hard he worried me. He was carrying a lot of weight, even for a big frame.

"I think we're all right now, Pug," I said, as I slowed to a walk. Pug passed me, then stopped and bent over, gasping for breath as he leaned on his carbine.

Just then the bandit shouted, "Y'all killed my little brother. I'm gonna gut every durn one of you!" I don't know if he was drunk or just slow to grasp things.

He crouched down and started toward us, but Pug's body blocked my shot. As I stepped sideways and raised my carbine, Pug stood and with one motion drew his revolver and whacked that bandit right across his face.

I heard his nose or cheekbone give away with a substantial crunch, and he spun away and went face down in the creek.

There was a lot of blood streaming away from his head downstream. I said, "I hope you ain't killed him." I laid down my carbine and said, "Cover me," as I pulled him out by his ankles.

I turned him over. "He ain't dead," I said, "but you did relieve him of one of his eyeballs."

"Not on purpose," Pug wheezed. "Must have been my front sight."

About then Ribeye yelled, "Is ever'thing all right? Can I come in now?"

I said, "Might as well, but keep an eye toward the fort. Squeak ain't here."

Pug took the one-eyed man's hat and poured cold creek water on his face. When he sat up and started hollering about his eye and nose, Pug said, "I didn't mean to take your eye, but you damn near gave me a heart attack and was charging me with this here knife. You make any more noise, and I'll pluck out the other eye."

That bandit could have been twenty-five or forty, short on hair, teeth, and clean clothes. Right scrawny, too.

Back at the cook fire the other bandit's head was burnt black, and his clothes was afire, but you could see that Ribeye's shot had blown out much of his forehead.

His brother said, "He's ruint. Can I pull him out?"

"Pull him out and put him out," I said. "There's water in that rain barrel. Then you can bury this other man. Y'all killed him?"

"Squeak did. Can I bury my brother, too?"

"No, sir. We'll take him with us to the fort, see is there paper on you two. You can tie him on a horse, but bury this poor bugger first."

Ribeye said, "That pork surely smells ready, and I am purely starved."

I said, "Go back and get your horse first."

Pug said, "I'll go get ours, Brodie. I can't stomach the smell of these pigs a minute longer. Maybe I'll wait for you upwind?"

"Good idea," I said. Turning to the bandit I said, "First thing, take the scarf off that dead farmer and wrap your head. Cover that eye socket, then put both bodies on horses. We'll lead 'em upwind and bury the farmer beyond this God-awful smell."

Ribeye said, "I'll just cut us off some of that pig whilst this boy loads up them bodies."

We joined Pug about two hundred paces north. The earth

was soft near the creek, and one hour later we were done with the digging.

"I'm the only one as knows Squeak," I said. "I guess I'm elected to ride into the fort and see can I corner him."

Pug said, "What if you meet him on the way?"

I said, "I've thought on that. Curly Jack wants him alive. I'll try to drop his horse and capture him, but it don't look to be too far from here to the fort."

"It ain't," said Ribeye.

"Well, then. Small chance I'll find him anywhere but at the bar in the sutler's store. In which case, I'll slip up behind and knock him on the head. And bring him back in chains, along with some soldiers to gather up these horses."

Pug just smiled and said, "Small chance."

I held up my claw and my hand and said, "What? What are you saying?"

He said, "It's another good plan. For the life of me, though, I cannot remember any plan surviving the first gunshot."

The bandit looked around and said, "Hey, can we go back and find my other eyeball? Maybe an army doctor can put it back in."

I said, "You'd have to fight some Cache Creek catfish for that eyeball."

That boy was several steps short of being truly slow.

Just then Ribeye blinked like he was coming out of a dream and said, "You know what I been thanking?"

Pug said, "Thanking who?"

Ribeye stared at him a moment, then said, "Naw, not that kind of thanking. I thank your plan might not work, Brodie. Want to know why?"

"Why, yes I do. Just what is it you think is wrong with it?"

"Well," he said, "he might spot you and run, if he didn't kill you first. You'd either chase him or be dead. Either way, we wouldn't have no idea what to do or which-a-way to head. No idea whatsoever. See what I mean?"

Pug said, "Faith, and he's right. We all need to go. Me and Ribeye will settle the horses with the army, whilst you turn in our one-eyed bandit and his dead friend. Maybe ask their provost if he's seen your man."

I could see they were right. "Y'all are right," I said. "Your plan is better 'n mine. Tie this boy's hands in front of him, and let's get started."

Pug said, "It's still just a plan."

I said, "Yeah, but it's a simple plan. They're the best kind. How come you need to worry me so, anyways?"

Chapter Sixteen

It was simple and it worked just perfect. Almost.

The ride in was as smooth as could be, what with a strong wind out of the west slinging tumbleweeds at us like giant bounding cannon balls, and some of our mounts was already spooky with that dead bandit flopping around.

Still and all, we made it. A guard steered Pug and Ribeye to the corral and pointed out the provost's office to me. Me and the bandit rode over.

I said, "Before you swing down, how 'bout you gaze around, see if you make out Squeak's horse?"

He gave the street a good look-see and said, "No, sir, he rides a fine looking pinto. Easy to spot. He ain't here."

We dismounted and tied off our horses and the one with his dead partner on it. I said, "One more thing. I need to know your name, Son."

He said, "That's it. How'd you come to know?"

"Know what?"

"My name. Well, it's really Jack Sturkie, same as my pa, but him and everybody else just called me Sonny, or Son."

I laughed and said, "Well, it don't matter what you was called before, I can guaran-damn-tee from now on you'll be known as One-Eyed Jack."

He looked confused for just a second, then said, "Yeah! Just like the playing card. Hot damn, that's a good one." He smiled all over his face, then pointed behind me. "Lookee there. It's

Squeak. Hey, Squeak!"

I was sort of slow to turn, thinking it was the old trick, but I didn't need to turn much to glimpse a fine looking pinto in the middle of the street, just as my prisoner stepped past me.

I tried to push Sturkie aside, but my claw got hooked in his suspenders, and then Squeak drew and fired twice. His first shot hit Sturkie in the neck and sprayed thick blood in my face and eyes.

His second shot hit Sturkie in the head and slammed him back into me. We went down in a tangle as Squeak kicked that pinto into a gallop straight down the street toward Ribeye, Pug, and our little horse herd.

I struggled to unhook from Sturkie, stand, and draw, but my eyes was blurred with his blood. Right then I heard Ribeye yell, "Is that him?!"

Squeak yelled back, "It's me!" then fired off two more rounds and hooked a left to disappear down a side street. I got off one shot then, but it was a flyer. Busted a hinge on a storm shutter, which failed to fall on Squeak's head and just swung down catty-whompus instead.

Ribeye was holding his leg and hollering, and Pug's horse was down. Pug pulled his carbine and ran to the side street but turned back to me and said, "He's gone."

I jabbed my hook toward Ribeye, and, when Pug moved to help him, I looked down on my prisoner, the former One-Eyed Jack Sturkie.

"Well," I said to his stone-dead body, "you have just set some kind of record for the shortest time of owning a good nickname." Squeak's second shot had hit him right square in his good eye.

I still wasn't sure if I was hit or not, as my eyes was some kind of messed up.

I said, "Pug, how bad is Ribeye?"

He said, "Oh, and he'll live. Shot through his calf, but it ain't spurting. What about you?"

"I ain't sure, but I can barely see. That boy can shoot, can't he? Take my horse and chase him." He nodded and was gone.

Soldiers swarmed us then and hustled me and Ribeye into their surgeon's office. He went to work on Ribeye's leg while his medico corporal washed out my eyes.

"You ain't hit none that I can see," he said, "but you do have some little bone fragments in your eyes. Bet it feels like sand, don't it?"

"More like rocks," I said. "Must've come off the back of Sturkie's skull."

"Your prisoner? Yeah, I looked at him. He didn't require no more attention from me whatsoever."

It was better than an hour before I could see much at all, and about then Pug came back. He was leading my pony. He found me on the porch of the medical office.

"He nearly foundered on me," he said. "My weight, you know. Didn't wish to kill your pony. Faith, now, your eyes look like you're coming off a five-day drunk."

"But you didn't kill him."

He said, "Not to worry on that, laddy. Never got a shot. He ran clean away. But tell me, was there paper on the dead boys?"

"No such luck," I said. "I wired home and the marshals' service in Fort Smith, too. Not a durn thing. And, to beat that, the army wants us to pay for the burials. And our getting patched up, too. It's a durn Yankee general running the fort here, that's what it is."

Pug laughed. "But you're all Yanks, are ye not? Just tack it on to the price of them Injun ponies."

We settled on the ponies the next day, and, since we wasn't soldiers, the army didn't care if me and Ribeye was fit to ride or not. We sold the Sturkie brothers' tack to the sutler for a few dollars but kept their mounts, one for Pug and the others as spares. This was looking to be a long pursuit. We rode west about noon.

The chase didn't last too long after all.

Chapter Seventeen

Ribeye picked up Squeak's trail where Pug had turned back.

"He's gonna pass south of the Wichita mountings. That's them off to the right front. I'm glad he ain't going in there."

Pug leaned over and whispered, "Surely he means 'mountains,' does he not?"

I nodded. To Ribeye I said, "Where you figure he's heading?"

"Me?" he said. "Was it me, I'd pick up the North Fork of the Red and make towards Mobeetie. Ain't no law there, so I hear."

He was right, I expect. Far as I knew, I was the last one to wear the badge there.

Second night out, maybe sixty miles northwest of Fort Sill, we was tracking him up the west side of the North Fork.

I said, "We ain't gaining on him, 'less he falters. We'll camp here."

"Not right here," Ribeye said. "They is a big storm coming. This river will surely rise. Let's go on up that little hill over there."

Pug said, "Sounds good to me. Hunker down in that dry wash and get out of this unending wind."

"Nope," said Ribeye. "Not there neither. If'n I'm right, this'll come a gully washer."

"Flash floods?" I could barely make out the rumble he was responding to.

"Yessir," he said. "I'm right sartain of it."

Pug looked at me and shrugged.

I said, "Well, if you're certain." I nudged my horse toward the hill.

"And not under that nice ol' oak, neither. It'll likely get lit up. And we orter hobble these horses."

We set up a slant canvas shelter and ate as the rumble got louder. It hit like a screaming terror soon after I got sound asleep.

Short of a tornado, ain't nothing much like a thunderstorm out on the plains. It's even more interesting at full dark. You can see the lightning for twenty, thirty miles all around, long as your eyes ain't full of driven sticks and dirt and rain.

Wind tore loose our shelter, and the three of us wound up huddled, sitting upright with that canvas wrapped around us. It took all our main strength to keep it from sailing away.

At some point, Ribeye muttered, "Leastways the lightning ain't as bad as I feared."

God must have been listening. Right then He sent a bolt down to that old oak tree, maybe forty yards away. It blew apart into a three-piece hulk, smoking and sizzling in the downpour.

Now, I don't know about Pug's big ass, but that strike bounced me and Ribeye right off that hard ground. Knocked down the mule and one horse, too. Broke the horse's leg. His screams got added to the uproar.

Pug said, "For mercy's sake, will somebody kill him?"

Ribeye said, "Kill him your own dang self."

Pug shouted, "You hold on to this canvas and I will!" I guess he had noticed that me and Ribeye kept losing our grip on it.

"I'll do it," I said. I tried to stand but got blown down right on my butt. I crawled near as I could with the horse kicking and trying to get up. It took two shots from my revolver to finish him.

I guess if we'd been closer and facing the river, we might of seen some of Squeak's gear float by. And maybe his body, too.

We found what was left of Squeak's camp, noon the next day. He had set up in a ravine and got washed away. His gear was strewn in a line right down to the river. His pinto was nearby, reins caught up in a scrub oak.

We found his blanket, tin cup, and carbine with a broke stock. And we found his saddle and saddle pockets. Inside was some socks, his mess tin, a little .38 Remington, and over eight hundred U.S. dollars, soaking wet. And beans, jerky, and canned tomatoes, of course.

"Boys," I said, "our work here is done. This here is most of what Squeak stole. We'll watch for his sorry butt as we go back down river, but we can head back to Texas."

Pug gazed away to the north and said, "Maybe not for me. How far to Canadian, do ye reckon?"

"Two, three days maybe," said Ribeye. "How come?"

"Sure, and me own dear cousin is there. I may never be so close again. I'm thinking I'm off for a visit, if you'll be so good as to ask Mister Sentell to take me off the payroll for a wee bit. And point me true."

Ribeye said, "Keep on a-going north and west. They's a good trail betwixt Mobeetie and Canadian, but do you miss it you'll soon hit the railroad tracks. Just turn right."

I pulled ten damp dollars from the recovered loot. "Curly owes you at least this much. If it's more, he'll square with you when you hook up again."

"And the captured horses we sold?"

I said, "Do it turn out we can't find relatives of them murdered Injuns and Mexicans, we'll split that even. You, me, and Ribeye."

He said, "Too fair. Go safely now," and he was gone.

Me and Ribeye didn't come up on Squeak's body on that slow trip back to the Ranger camp. Didn't seem to matter, as we had got back most of the thousand Squeak had stole from Curly Jack. And we was upright. I don't mean virtuous. As a posse, we was limping, sore, and part blind, but we was vertical. And, far as we knew, Squeak wasn't.

Chapter Eighteen

Heading back to the Red River crossing, Ribeye put us on an angle that cut off a bunch of travel. We passed right far to the south and west of Fort Sill and that little hog farm where we had caught the horse thieves.

Didn't do us much good anyways, as that rainstorm had swollen the river too much to even try a crossing for a couple of days. Time it went down we had missed the whole shindig over to College Station.

Curly Jack, Wade, Miz Sentell, and Emmalee came in by train the day after me and Ribeye got back to Wichita Falls. Curly had sent a wire to the station telling us when they'd get in, on the off chance we had completed our mission.

Wade spotted us as they pulled up and was off the train before it come to a full stop. He was busting wide open with excitement.

"You shoulda been there, Pop. We stayed in a real nice house and got to tour the whole school like we was royal dukes or something."

"Tour?"

"That's what they called it, Pop. It means you get to see everything just like you owned it. And that ain't the best thing, neither. The general talked to me about the law, and he give me a whole durn set of law books."

I said, "Whoa. Law books?"

"Yessir. Said I can study on my own and take the test

whenever I's ready."

Curly interrupted us just then. Now, you might think he would of taken a minute to tell us what a grand time we missed. Well, not so much.

"Where's Squeak?" he demanded. "You got him in the jail?"

"No sir," I said. "He's . . ."

"Don't be telling me you killed him, Dent. I tole you don't kill him."

Miz Sentell cut in on him just then and said, "John, you let that young man hug his wife hello before you go on so about business. You get us settled into the hotel and started on some hot baths, then you can find out what Brodie knows over a drink."

Curly muttered, "Yes ma'am. Ribeye, you and Wade grab some of these layabouts and get the women and baggage to the hotel. Brodie, let's have that drink and see how you managed to mess this up."

I said, "Before you say another word or take another step, you need to know we got back maybe eight hundred of your dollars that Squeak stole. And he got away."

"Well, Sweet Jesus, Brodie. Why didn't you say so? Come on. I'm buying."

I got to hug Emmalee later.

Back at the LT spread, life settled in to a sort of comfortable routine. Wade was deep into his law books, with lots of help from Emmalee and Miz Sentell. And Curly, believe it or not. He would tell Wade about some dust-up he'd been in, then between them they'd try to figure out what the legal outcome was. Or might have been, if Curly hadn't of shot the criminals.

"Alleged criminals," Wade would say. "The fact that you shot them don't prove they was guilty."

Curly snorted. "If they wasn't guilty, why would I shoot 'em?

Go ahead. Nary a one was innocent. You prove otherwise, and I'll kiss your butt on the front porch steps on Sunday morning."

That was a fairly safe bet. In those olden days, it was hard to find anybody totally innocent anywhere near Curly. Including him.

As for me, I had to spend my days and maybe half my nights over at the Ranger camp. Served some papers, chased some thieves, pulled night watch and such, but then my sergeant got me to ride with him to check out reports of a rogue longhorn, one county west of us. This steer was supposed to be terrorizing innocent citizens out riding and had rammed at least one wagon.

We found him easy enough, or maybe he found us. He come out of some bushes snorting fire and ran slam into the sergeant's horse. Head butted that bay, right in the chest. The bay stayed on his feet and spun away but threw the sergeant. The longhorn turned on me, and I put three pistol balls in his head and shoulder. I would say my shooting didn't faze him, but he did thunder off, back into them bushes, never to be seen again.

My sergeant was one unhappy mess. Since we was expecting trouble, all six of his cylinders was loaded, and that holstered Colt went off right down his thigh when he hit the ground. Broke his leg, and it's a good bet, if I hadn't been there, he would have bled out. I made him a good tourniquet with his scarf and pistol barrel, got him back in the saddle, and we was home before midnight. He was later discharged as a cripple.

Anyways, Curly leaned on the Ranger captain to promote me. What with the Cane Pole Jack story and Curly's friendship with General/Governor/President Ross floating around, the captain thought my promotion was a pretty good idea. Which allowed me a little more time at the ranch with Emmalee, and a nice pay raise.

Even Curly seemed to relax, and then, maybe two months after we last saw him, Pug showed up.

Me, the Sentells, Ribeye, Pug, and Emmalee was sitting in rockers on the Sentells' porch. Wade was inside studying.

"My cousin has a bloody school in Canadian, started by he himself," Pug said. "All the wee ones attend, as well as a number of big hairy grown-ups."

I said, "Them as ain't got their numbers or letters yet, I guess?"

"Just as you say. And some as do, hoping to improve their lot. Now, my dear relative don't wear the garb of a priest no more, but he does hold a small service Sundays in his school house, for any as claims to be Catholic. Or anyone else, for that matter. I mean there's not no other church anywhere near."

Curly said, "How come he quit dressing the part?"

Pug grinned. "Well, there's that, too, isn't there? Another reason to let you non-papist heathens into his services? He really is no longer a priest. He was kicked out of the priesthood by Mother Church after he kicked hell out of a priest for bothering wee boys. Faith, now, and isn't that a twist?"

"The church's loss, and good for him," Curly snorted. He banged his fist on the table beside him, startling everybody and near knocking over Miz Sentell's lemon water.

She tut-tutted and pulled a hanky from her bodice to wipe up the spill. Looking over at me, she winked and said softly, "Here he goes."

"I'm sorry, Missus, but I feel strongly on this. I've decided the durn Injuns is right. A man, or a woman for that matter, can choose whether they like men or women, and I ain't even sure they has a real choice. What I'm dead sure of is that small children cain't choose nothing. I see, or even hear of some grown-up messing with a child, they go to Curly's Court."

I'm not sure I ever heard Curly say that much about anything, leastways not in one breath.

Pug raised his eyebrows and said, "Curly's Court? And, Lord love a duck, are you a justice too?"

"I am not," said Curly, "but I'm for it. Justice, I mean. I find them guilty, and I punish them."

"Punish is right," I said. "He executes them, more likely as not."

"Yessir," Curly said. "Some crimes don't call for no second chances."

If anyone who ever heard Curly's thoughts on that subject disagreed with him, I never heard it. Not then nor later.

Pug just nodded and said, "A man after me own heart. Now, I do have some news that may interest you. It's about Squeak."

There was a flurry of chatter, but Curly stopped rocking and said, "Y'all hush up. Let's hear it."

"I returned by way of Mobeetie," said Pug. "Seems Squeak passed through a week or so before me, riding a mule. Bareback, probably stole. We shared, uh, drinks with the same woman, and I questioned her enough that I'm fair certain it was him."

"He still there?" Me and Curly asked the same question at the same time.

"He is not," Pug answered. "He met a man he'd met before. They traded mounts and rode south together. The woman said they was heading for Jacksboro."

Curly stood. "Let's get some provisions and mount up."

Pug held up both hands. "I can tell you they are not there, leastways not yesterday. I rode straight there. Found Lord Jim in a Monte game, and he said they'd passed through last week."

"Going whichaways?" Curly's face was near black with anger, and danged if he didn't check the loads in his Schofield.

"Lord Jim weren't sure, but they was trying to recruit a gang to come after you and your money. Said he thought they struck out for Weatherford and maybe Fort Worth."

I said, "How many with him?"

"Just one, so far. Lord Jim said he was called Muley. Muley Lee-something-or-other."

"I will be damned," I said. "Muley Lefevre."

"Got to be," chimed in Ribeye. "Remember? Squeak and him connected over to Plainview, afore we caught up to Muley."

"They could be anywheres now," I said.

"Don't matter none," Curly said. "We'll head for Weatherford come morning."

"I don't see no problem," I said, "but I do have to go by the camp. Brief the captain, get Pug on the payroll, make sure we can take Ribeye. And Pug."

"No need," Curly said. "I'll go telephone the captain now. He'll see things my way. I told you a wire to that camp was a good investment. Another thing, O'Hanley. I ain't pleased to be supported by a man with a single-shot carbine."

I said, "Well, maybe you can trade up when we gets to Weatherford, Pug. I owe you your share of the sale of them ponies up at Fort Sill. We tried but never could find nobody name of A. Chavez. Not one who was missing, leastways."

Ribeye laughed. "Yep, they was a couple of Mexes or breeds by that name as showed up to claim their riches, but, when Brodie tole 'em they had to be dead for it to be rightfully theirs, they just give up on the spot and rode off."

I said, "That's a happy fact. Another thing, though, Curly. You owe Pug whatever wages he has coming, above the ten I paid him."

Curly Jack give us this sly smile and said, "I make that to be about twelve dollars more. I'll give it to you in trade, O'Hanley. Now lemme go make that call."

Chapter Nineteen

In what was no surprise to anyone but maybe Pug, my captain agreed a hundred percent with Curly Jack.

Me, Curly, Pug, and Ribeye rode out the next morning. Pug was toting Curly's old '76 Winchester, a repeater known as Sally Ann. Didn't seem as neither Pug nor Curly was displeased with Pug's improved hardware. I said so to Pug as he rode beside me.

He shrugged. "Sure, and it's a puny cartridge compared to a .577 round. But even a thick-headed Irishman can see the advantage of being able to deliver five or six shots in the time it would take to fire me dear old Snyder twice."

Curly gave one of his disgusted snorts and twisted in his saddle to look back at Pug. "Puny? That .45-75 will knock over a buffalo, or mule, or man just as fine as one of your old fat, slow English bullets. Throw its slug farther and flatter, too. Puny? Horse droppings, I say. You'll see."

Pug laughed, rich and full. "Sure, and who am I to distrust the word of Master Curly Jack Sentell, Lord of the Western Plains? And a known killer of buffaloes, mules, and men?"

Curly stared at him a moment, then grinned. "You got that right, Irishman. Tell you what. Let's hold up here a minute. There's a fat jackrabbit off to the left there. Whyn't you see can you hit it with that puny carbine I give you?"

Pug unshucked Sally Ann, aimed, and fired. Turned out he was a fair shooter.

"Jaysus!" Pug shook his head, staring at his smoking carbine and then at his target. Wasn't much left but ears, feet, and fur.

Curly kicked his horse into moving again. Over his shoulder, he said, "Private O'Hanley. Known killer of bunny rabbits."

O'Hanley made a funny face, then said, "Sure, Marshal Sentell, and you must tell me about the Keep Ranch fight. Brodie says that you was in it, but he didn't provide no details."

"Brodie weren't more'n sixteen back in February '71 and weren't nowhere near the Keep Ranch. What details could he give?"

"Ten of you against forty hostiles, he said. He never said how many of you survived."

Curly pulled his hat and scratched his head, something he often did to help remember details. "Every one of us made it, though one boy was hurt bad. They was forty-one of them, and they had two chiefs, one Comanche and one Kioway. Oska Horseback and Sittanke, they was named. We killed both chiefs plus five others. Wounded several more. Caught 'em butchering a stolen beef and fought near about three hours afore sending 'em back to the Territory, tails between their legs. And marvelous tales to tell, too, just like us. See, the state of Texas had give our whole company '66 Winchesters. Had more'n forty rounds each, plus our pistols. Ten of us was aplenty for all of them, even though they had some guns, and was slinging arrows like crazy. Reminded me of a mad whore throwing rocks, they did."

Curly paused then. That was a lot of gab, coming from him. We didn't mind none, as we was facing a long ride, and the talk seemed to eat up miles.

I said, "One day, Curly, you got to tell me that story. The one about the mad whore, that is."

He smiled. "Deputy, that day will never come."

Ribeye said, "I always wondered did maybe you-all go up against the same gang of Injuns as wiped out that darky Britton

Johnson and his teamsters along the Butterfield Stage Route. It was around the same time, and weren't too far away."

"I'm fair certain they was a different gang. That two weeks afore our fight, and they was thought to be all Kioway. Chief was Maman-Ti or something like that. Now, in that fight, Nigger Britt had a Yellowboy carbine, like us, and he hurt 'em bad afore they killed him. Over seventy spent cartridges inside, and at least twelve gouts of blood outside his little fort."

Pug said, "He was in a fort?"

Curly laughed. "Sort of. He was found in betwixt some of his dead mules. Made hisself a kind of fort. That Negro was a piece of work, I'm here to tell you. Freed slave, smart, had his own freight business, and hard as a railroad spike. Kioway had raided his home back in '64 whilst he was away, killed some of his family and captured the rest. He made about four trips up into the Nations to get back his wife and one daughter."

Ribeye said, "Some of the old marshals I worked with knew of Johnson from his trips into the Territory. Said the Kioway hated him and hoped to catch him alone. I think he fought them until he run slam out of cartridges. Then, of course, they gutted him and stuck his own dog in his stomach hole. It was already dead, of course."

Curly smiled. "Of course. Something else about them days y'all should know. When I rode with the Rangers, I was traveling under a different moniker. It weren't for certain that old Rebels was allowed yet. That, and there was a dispute with a woman over a child."

That took me aback. "You left a wife and child?"

"We weren't married, Brodie, thank you very much, and the child was a redhead. Woman had three evil brothers who didn't take into account that I had a full head of black hair back then."

I said, "What name did you use?"

"I won't say, but it was not the same as I used when I rode

with Custer's cavalry. Plenty of reasons to change who you was back then. The Seventh U.S. Cavalry might still be looking for a deserter name of Corporal Jack Smith. I just got fed up with the 'boy general' after the Washita fight, and left."

Pug grinned and said, "Lot of that going around."

Ribeye said, "I don't know how you two remember who you is."

Chapter Twenty

We stopped at a small ranch to water the horses, but nobody was home. Chickens and a dog, one milk cow, but no horses or mules. And no wagon. We helped ourselves at the well and rode on. Curly pointed out a fresh grave on a nearby hill.

Wasn't long before we overtook a wagon on the Weatherford road. Wasn't hard to do either, as it was halted dead still. A man was unhitching the mule while a woman took turns yelling at him and sobbing. Three children stood in the wagon.

As we closed up, they all stopped what they was doing and stared at us.

Curly tipped his hat and said, "Ma'am."

The woman nodded, wiped her nose, and said, "Yessir?"

Curly stared at the man but kept speaking to the woman. "You all right here, missus?"

The man said, "Y'all just ride on. This ain't none of your business."

Curly smiled and said, "I might could make it so."

The woman said, "No, sir, we ain't all right. This man is trying to steal our mule."

"Ain't hers," the man said. "It's mine. Her man took it, and I'm taking it back."

Her eyes flashed like lightning. "He's a liar. My husband bought it from him. Now my Odell is dead, and this no-account is a-trying to take advantage of me."

Curly swung down and stretched.

"I ain't doing no such," the man said. "Just taking what's rightly mine." To my mind, he was right whiney.

Curly jabbed a finger at him. "You shut up. Even if it's yours, you was gonna leave her and her kids out here? I'll talk to you directly, but for now you just close your pie hole."

Turning to the widow, Curly said, "What happened to your man?" It always took me by surprise when Curly spoke soft.

"He was murdered last week," she said. "Somebody shotgunned him down by the road. I think it was him." She glared at the man.

"It was him, Mama. I seen it. I told you already," said the oldest child, a girl maybe twelve.

"You ain't seen shit, you little lying bitch. I'll tell you—"

Curly cut him off by back-handing him with his Schofield. The man grunted and sat down, blood pouring from his nose.

Curly bent over him. "You feel better now? You reckon you can hold your filthy tongue, or do I need to stick some more of your teeth through it?"

The man nodded, eyes wide and full of fear.

Curly turned back to the woman. "That your place we passed a while back?"

"Yessir," she sobbed. "I sent for the law, but the sheriff's deputy is this man's kin. Won't do nothing. Now he'll prob'ly come and take the mule."

The man groaned and stood up. "I think you done busted my nose." He started toward his horse.

Pug pointed Sally Ann at him and said, "One more step, my dandy, and we'll all see how hard this thing hits. And what might your name be?"

The man stared into the mouth of Sally Ann. His own mouth moved, but nothing came out.

"He's one of them Clintons," the widow said. "Trash. Pig farmers."

Pug grinned. "Oh, and I should have known. Now, would that be a shotgun in your saddle scabbard, Boyo?"

It was. Curly walked over, pulled the double-barrel, and carried it to the wagon. He handed it up to the oldest boy. Could have been ten. "Check the loads, Son. Don't give it back to him."

The boy said, "Yessir," then cracked the breech. "Loaded," he said, then slammed it closed. And cocked it.

"Clinton," Curly said, "we're gonna have a 'Come to Jesus' minute, right here, right now. Pay attention."

Curly broke open his Schofield and emptied the cartridges into his other palm. He closed it, cocked it, and handed it to Clinton. "Try that trigger, Mister Clinton. Go right on. You seen me empty it."

Clinton touched the trigger, and the hammer snapped down on the empty chamber. He jumped. "Judas Priest," he said. "Hair-triggered."

Curly said, "Yessir, that's just how I like it." He took it back, reloaded it, and cocked it again. "Now open your mouth." He put the barrel against Clinton's lips.

Clinton froze, then started to shake his head.

Curly said, "Don't do that, boy. You bump this thing, and it'll go off. Open your mouth. I won't ask you again."

Clinton slowly opened his mouth, and Curly poked the muzzle in past the man's teeth.

"Give me a thumbs-up if you sold this family this mule. Don't budge, less you want a new mouth in the back of your head."

Thumbs-up.

"Thumbs-up if you killed their daddy. You can try a thumbs-down, if you choose to lie, but you need to know I done made up my mind which party exactly is in the wrong here."

Another thumbs-up. Slower, this time.

"Well, there you have it, Brodie. A clear confession in front of a Ranger sergeant." Curly withdrew his muzzle from the man's mouth, de-cocked his revolver, and turned back toward us.

He didn't make it two steps before the shotgun blast startled us all. Mostly it startled Clinton, who took the buckshot load in the stomach and sat down again. He stared at the blood on his grubby white shirt and gasped for breath.

I know I should have seen it coming, and I guess it should bother me to this day. I mean, I seen that boy cock that shotgun. I try and I try, but I still can't seem to give a damn. As my heart slid back down out of my throat, we all turned toward the boy standing in the wagon.

As the smoke cleared a little, he fired again. The second load took Clinton in the head. He was slammed flat. He only twitched twice.

Curly was the first to speak. "Clear case of suicide," he said. "Must have been eat up with guilt. Brodie, you can report it to this man's kin. You know, that deputy. See that he don't bother these folks."

"I'll talk to him, Curly, but I can fairly say this was like attempted horse theft. That's a hanging crime. Mule theft is even worse. The boy was legal to shoot him."

Curly remounted. "Whatever you say, Sergeant Dent. Y'all sling him on his horse. And get that mule back in his traps, so's we can escort these folks on into town."

As Pug helped the widow back up to her wagon seat, he said, "Faith, and you've just witnessed a Curly Court. Was it not a grand thing?"

Chapter Twenty-One

We tied Mister Clinton's horse to the tail end of the wagon, with his hands and ankles lashed to his stirrups. Curly Jack and Ribeye took the lead, while me and Pug rode alongside the wagon.

I could have drifted back and traveled beside or behind the recent Mister Clinton, but I didn't favor eating dust no more than anyone else. So I wasn't there just trying to hear what Pug and the widow had to say to one another.

Still, it wasn't too boring.

"I didn't catch your name back there," Pug said.

"Didn't give it," she said. "It's Boyte."

Pug grinned. "Faith, now, that's a new one on me. Boyte what?"

"That's our last name. It's German. Papa was German. You don't know much, do you?" That came from her oldest boy. Younger one might have been five or six and didn't have much to say.

Pug lifted his hat and swabbed his forehead, then stared at the boy.

"You just shot down an unarmed man in front of three Texas Rangers, laddie. You might wish to watch your words until we testify in your behalf."

"They is four of you," the boy said. If he was scared of Pug, it didn't show. "You only said three."

Ribeye piped up. "Only three is Rangers. The old bald one

there used to Ranger some and soldier some, too, but he's best known as a lawman, afore he married rich."

Over his shoulder, Curly said, "Thin ice, Private Johnson. Precious thin."

"Rebekah," the widow said. "I'm Rebekah Boyte. And he's Karl. Karl, with a *K*. And with his papa's mouth. Don't mind him too much. He's not yet eleven."

"Well, then," Pug said. "And may I now call you Rebekah?"

"Since I don't know none of your names or your friends, you'd best stick to Missus Boyte."

"Ah, fair enough. I'm Pug O'Hanley, on your other side is Sergeant Brodie Dent, and up front is Curly Jack Sentell and Private Ribeye Johnson. And now may I call you Becky?"

"We'll see. I doubt I'll know you long enough to get that familiar."

"A hard woman," Pug said. "Well, Missus Boyte, why are you going to Weatherford?"

"I don't know as that's none of your business," she said.

I could see Pug was taking more than a passing interest in this particular widow, so I took a closer look myself.

She was anywhere from thirty to forty, not heavy, but bulging in the right places. Face was weathered, but she had good features with high cheekbones, blue eyes, and I wished I could see her smile.

"None of our business, you say. And did we not just save your mule?" Pug shook his head. "And are we not, even now, riding to make certain your boy isn't hung for murder?"

She shrugged and said, "If you has to know, we're on our way to buy some breeding stock."

"Breeding stock? You mean to raise cattle? Where?"

The daughter said, "Maybe you seen our ranch house, but you ain't rode our range yet. We got a right smart piece of land. Plenty to run cattle on, even with all the durn clay. Water, too.

Two good streams, one of 'em feeding a pond where Papa and Karl dammed it up."

Pug said, "How big is the spread?"

"Maybe three thousand acres," Karl said.

Pug whistled. The widow's glare could've cut her son in two.

Karl said, "Yeah, but at least five hundred is clay. Red clay."

"That's what the bloody English use to make bricks," Pug said.

I said, "What, red bricks? That's what Miz Sentell wants. A big durn red-brick house, that won't catch fire every time some cook loses his temper. Ain't that right, Curly?"

Curly was riding on ahead and said, "Do what?" I had to repeat myself.

"Well," he said, "it ain't burnt up yet, leastways not complete. And my bride's wants and wishes ain't likely to kill her."

The daughter said, "There must be a passel more like her. A man done come from the other side of Jacksboro to try and buy a section of our clay land for a brick-making company. Papa was thinking on it when he was murdered."

Pug said, "Maybe your mother ought to sell. You could move to Weatherford or Fort Worth."

Missus Boyte said, "I was born on that farm. Papa died in the war, and both brothers, too. It passed to me when Mama died. I won't sell. I'll eat armadillos first."

Ribeye finally joined in. "Y'all know why God made armadillos? So poor folk could have possum on the half shell."

The widow stared at him like he had just made water on her front porch.

Ribeye said, "You know, like them oysters at that big hotel in Fort Worth."

Curly snorted. "I don't know nobody as eats 'em. Not even Tonkawas."

Ribeye said, "Possums or oysters? I've eat a mess of both of 'em."

"No, you idjit, I'm speaking of armadillos. It's a good thing you can track, as otherwise you're just tiring out a good horse. You ain't got nary brain in your head."

The talk amongst us went on like that, all the way to Weatherford. There the wagon rattled and wobbled over the train tracks as we hit the edge of town.

Pug said, "Miz Boyte, may I help you pick out your breeding stock?"

"I'm just a poor widow. I ain't helpless nor stupid."

"Faith, and I meant no such thing. It's just that some men might try to take advantage. Men like Clinton, back there."

Her blue eyes flashed. "And my family dealt with that, did we not?"

Pug made a strange face, held up both hands, and turned toward me. "There's no being nice to her, is there now?"

Her daughter said, "Mama, don't be so ill. He's only trying to help."

The oldest boy said, "Yeah, and it ain't like he's drunk, neither. Not like Papa always was."

Rebekah Boyte frowned at her son, for sharing that tidbit I'd guess. But then she softened, right in front of our eyes.

"I shouldn't ought to have spoke to you so, Mister O'Hanley. Least not in such a way." She struggled and forced a smile.

Did I tell you this was a dark, overcast day? Pug lit up right then like the heavens had opened and splashed sunshine directly on him.

Curly shifted in his saddle, looked back, and said, "Don't none of it matter. We got business to attend to. Can't be sending no Ranger to help buy no dang-blasted cows."

I guess we was all tired and strung out. I should've made al-

lowance for that, but what Curly said truly pissed me off.

"I'll ride with the Boytes to see them settled," I snapped. "Pug, you come with me, case that deputy and his friends don't understand we want her left alone."

Curly wasn't at all used to any back talk. He must've seen how wrong he was.

"Good idea, Brodie. Me and Ribeye will do a scout and meet you two by that bar near the train station." He turned away and muttered, "Don't dally."

Chapter Twenty-Two

As Curly and Ribeye rode off, Mrs. Boyte said, "What you want me to do with this body?"

I said, "Swing by the town marshal's office, and we'll drop him there. Y'all can go on about your business while me and Pug talk to the law about your particular situation."

She said, "They ain't taking my boy. Not without a fight. He only did what's right." She looked at Pug. "You tell them."

Pug nodded, and I said, "Yes'm. That's what we will be explaining to them. Now, this deputy, the one you worry about. He named Clinton, too?"

"No, sir," said the boy. "He's a Satterwhite."

"Mostly the Satterwhites is good people," the widow added. "This here deputy is a black sheep. Don't be a-turning your back on him."

I nodded. "We won't. Now tell me about the marshal."

She said, "He's all right, but getting on up there in age. Might be fifty. He's a Lucas and was in the war with my Odell, long afore we was married. Satterwhite just takes advantage of his trusting nature. And here comes his office, ahead over to your left."

"Pull over there, right in front."

She did and stamped on the brake. Her boy Karl had reloaded the shotgun and was fidgeting with the hammers.

Me and Pug swung down, and both of us unshucked our long guns. We walked to Clinton's horse and cut the rope on his wrists and ankles. Pug grabbed ahold of the dead man by his feet and tipped the body over into the dusty street.

Looking up at the boy, Pug said, “Now, laddie, don’t speak a word unless I ask you, and don’t cock that cannon unless things get tense. Clear?”

Karl nodded, then cocked both barrels. “Things is tense,” he said, staring at the office door.

I walked up the two steps to the boardwalk just as the door opened and two men came out. Both wore badges, and one was white-haired. I faced him.

“You Lucas?”

“I am,” he said, “and who might you be?”

“Sergeant Brodie Dent, Texas Rangers. The big man there is Ranger O’Hanley. I’m pleased to meet you, so far.” I held my carbine with my hook and stuck out my right hand.

He gave me a firm shake and said, “Heard of you. Used to be Mobeetie law. Who’s the body? I trust that ain’t your Odell, Miz Rebekah, is it?”

She shook her head, and I said, “Her Odell is dead, but this dead man is a horse thief name of Clinton. Related to one of your deputies, I’m told.” I shifted my focus and the barrel of my carbine toward the deputy.

“Satterwhite here is my only deputy, so I’m guessing that there is Willy Clinton.”

Clinton wasn’t totally recognizable, what with his face mostly shot off. The deputy didn’t show much interest in the deceased before I named him, but then he hurried down to stare at the body.

“It is Willy,” he said, “but he weren’t no horse thief.”

Pug smiled. “It was Willy, though he ain’t Willy no more, is he now? And he tried to steal a mule. I’m told you Yanks find that worse than horse thievery. It was that mule, right there, Boyo. And we witnessed it.”

"We stopped it," I said, "and he admitted it, before he, uh, died."

"Died, hell. Y'all murdered him." Satterwhite tried to draw his pistol, but Pug swung that big Winchester sideways against the deputy's forearm.

I'm right certain I heard it crack, but anyways the man dropped his revolver, and I didn't have to shoot him. Pug kicked the gun away and then kicked the man between his legs. He went to his knees and made some funny noises.

Soon as Pug hit the man, I switched back to the marshal. His thumbs was hooked in his suspenders, and all he did was look disgusted.

I said, "Marshal Lucas, I'm arresting him for attempted assault on a Ranger. Any problem?"

"No sir," he said, "I seen it myself. He ain't never been worth spit, but I couldn't never catch him at nothing serious. And wouldn't nobody testify against him neither. Nor even run against him."

"He kilt my husband, too. Clinton, that is, not your deputy. My daughter seen it. But I sent you word, and Satterwhite come out and wouldn't do nothing. Said I couldn't even prove my Odell was dead, what with him shot in the face, just like Clinton there."

"I am sorry, Miz Rebekah. I wasn't told. You know I liked Odell when he wasn't drunk. How come you tried to take her mule, Satterwhite?"

Satterwhite still couldn't get words out. The widow said, "He claimed it was still his'n, but it weren't. He sold it to my Odell."

The marshal lifted his hat and scratched his head. "You got a bill of sale?"

Pug interrupted before she could answer. "She does, in fact. Saw it with me own eyes. No need for her to show it again."

The widow and me both stared at Pug. I don't know about

her, but I clean missed that part where she showed us a bill of sale. Turned out it didn't matter.

"Well, all right then. A Ranger's word is good enough for me. We'll put him in my jail. Judge ought to be sober by tomorrow, and we can finally put his no-account butt away."

About then Satterwhite recovered enough to say, "Hey, wait. You can't—"

Pug whacked him with Sally Anne alongside his head, and he went down for the count.

Marshal Lucas smiled and said, "Yes, we can. We surely can."

Chapter Twenty-Three

We was having breakfast in the hotel next morning. Turned out that the Weatherford lawman was able to help us some with our pursuit.

"Squeak and his man Muley left here last week, Wednesday I believe it was. They's a-riding towards Abilene."

Curly scratched his bald noggin. "Riding, you say. They didn't take the train?"

The marshal nodded. "Would've been faster, I'll grant you. They said they was a-meeting up with some compadres over to Mineral Wells. Gonna take the water a while afore heading on to Abilene."

Ribeye said, "Take the water?"

"Yessir," said the marshal.

"Take it where?"

"Oh," the marshal laughed, "I clean forgot all of you ain't from around here. I meant they planned to take the treatment over there. Mineral waters. You soak in 'em. And they surely needed it, as they was both still half drunk when they rode out."

Curly said, "Well, you managed to get an awful lot of information out of 'em."

"We had plenty of time. They spent that last night here in my jail on account of raucous and rude behavior."

"Say they did. And I thought they was such nice boys." Curly laughed.

"No, sir. Not nice, not them two. Squeak insulted the madam

over to the Golden Dove, and then Muley insulted me. I had to go upside his head with my shotgun butt to calm him down. And my deputy stroked Squeak across the bridge of his nose, to mellow him out."

"What did he use?" Curly was always right interested in whacking, him being such a believer in it. "Bet it was that solid frame Merwin Hulbert we took off him last night."

"It surely was," said the marshal. "Good pistol for buffaloing surly drunks. I believe I'll keep it."

Curly pushed back from the table and said, "You've been a powerful aid, Sheriff. I guess the upshot of all this is that if we catch the Fort Worth to Abilene train, we just might catch 'em there."

"You just might beat 'em. But you needs to move quick, else you'll miss that train. And be cautious, do you catch up to them. Squeak's got one of them new slide-action shotguns. Must hold five shells or better. And it's sawed off."

It was just over one hundred miles to Abilene. Maybe four days by horse or mule, but less than a day by train. We was about halfway there when it happened.

The train had already slowed considerable, pulling a long hill in some heavy woods. There was a card game in our car, a penny a point and a quarter a set, so way too rich for dog-ass poor Rangers. The three of us watched as Curly Jack played, but then the train lurched and jolted to a dead stop.

The conductor pushed past me to see what the problem was, mumbling, "Sorry, folks, but we ain't supposed to stop hereabouts."

He stepped off the train, then jumped right back on and shouted, "Holdup! It's a durn holdup. They got trees across the track. Three of 'em, horseback, up to the mail car."

Ribeye was closest to the door and first one past the unarmed conductor and out the door. Pug was next, but he caught his spurs in somebody's baggage strap and went down, blocking the aisle.

I jumped over him, nearly, but come down on his right hand. His gun hand, of course. Pug yelled and tried to rise just as Curly went to step over him, and they went down in a tangle.

I almost stopped to help, but then Ribeye shouted something outside, so I went on and jumped out, too. There was some kind of rocky embankment down to a ditch, and my feet went out from under me. I had my carbine clutched in my right hand, and my claw wasn't any help in stopping my slide.

I was on my left side though, facing uphill, so I saw the whole thing, even as I slid. Squeak was off his horse, holding the baggage clerk or mailman or whatever he was at the point of his shotgun. There was one more passenger car between us and the mail car. No question it was Squeak, bandaged nose and all.

Ribeye was easing toward Squeak, holding onto the train with his left hand and pointing his revolver with the other. I believe he yelled, "Give it up!" and he had the drop on Squeak. Squeak knew it, too. He started to lower his shotgun, but then Ribeye seemed to notice the citizens gawking out the windows. He raised both hands toward them, like to push them back, and yelled, "You all set yourselves down and keep your heads inside."

Like a flash, Squeak raised his barrel and fired. Ribeye's hat flew back towards me, and there was blood spray off his head. He sort of bounced off the side of the passenger car and pitched down the embankment headfirst, just as I yelled and Squeak fired at me.

I don't know that Ribeye put himself between me and and that second load of buckshot on purpose, or if God did it, but that's what happened. And if the first load of buckshot didn't kill him, the second one surely did. One pellet grazed my shoulder, and another dented the can on my arm, but Ribeye took the rest of them in his left side. Yessir. The heart side. He was dead when he slid facedown into the ditch.

I purely despised Squeak up to this point, but what he did next turned my heart to stone-cold hate.

There was a bunch of passengers still leaning and looking out the windows of both passenger cars. Shouldn't of been, but they was. Squeak shucked that slide-action twice and fired the next two loads right at them.

Right down the side of the train. It wasn't no accident, neither. He hit seven men and one woman and two children, what with all the buckshot, ricochets, and flying glass. Could have killed them all. It is a pure wonder that only three died.

Squeak jumped into the ditch where Muley was holding his horse and was remounting when I finally sat up and got off two shots. Don't know if I hit Squeak or his little Appaloosa, but they staggered some, both of them. At that moment, Curly stepped into the door of our car, took one look, and fired. That .50-110 was as loud as Squeak's shotgun, and the slug knocked Squeak's pony down. All that caused Muley's big mule and the third man's horse to do some dancing, which spoiled their aim. A good thing, too, as both of the men was firing pistols at me and Curly.

Pug shoved Curly off the train just then, and Curly hit the loose stone like me. He sat on his butt and slid down the bank, right into me, so as we wound up in a jumble.

Squeak fired again, this time at Pug, but Pug must have seen that sawed-off gun swing towards him. He was still on the steps of the train door. He ducked back and only took one ricochet pellet in the jaw. It did knock loose one tooth.

Me and Curly was trying to get untangled, but I heard Squeak just then. Heard him clear, even with all the screaming and hollering from wounded passengers and horses.

He said, "Muley, get down and give me your mule."

Muley looked right astonished. Despite the smoke, I seen it just as clear as I had heard Squeak's demand. Muley shook his head, and Squeak blasted him right out of his saddle, then climbed aboard himself and thundered off into the woods.

The third man had pushed his horse between us and Squeak to cover him, I suppose. Pug and Curly both got off shots just then. One round killed the horse, and the other hit the man in the side of his head. They went down together.

Curly sent one more round after Squeak, then said, "Neither one of them boys paid no attention as to how Squeak rewarded loyalty, did they?" I guess he was still mad about Squeak stealing from him and Missus Sentell, after years of being employed by the LT spread.

Our ditch was right full. Two dead horses and three dead men. Never did learn for sure who the third man was. Curly said he was wanted for murder and was J. E. Holder, known as "Black Face" cause of a powder burn on his left cheek from a rifle exploding on him. Problem was that Curly shot him in his right cheek and blew off the other side of his face. Made identification inconclusive, in my opinion. Curly said he was certain he seen the mark before he shot it off. Said we'd go on and claim any bounty on Holder, anyways.

Nobody argued with him.

I'd like to say we dusted off, got our own horses off the train, and lit out after Squeak. That didn't happen. We did get our horses off, but it was to help get those trees off the track.

Seems like Squeak must have fired that shotgun again as he rode off, 'cause when we did dust off, each of us had been hit some. Pug had his mouth still bleeding pretty good, but he had took two more pellets in his left leg and a pistol ball through his other calf. Curley had two pellets in his left thigh. One had cut up my right forearm, and another had gouged my left knee and bounced off the bone. Hurt like all hell, once I noticed it.

No more chasing for us for a while. Once we cleared the trees away, we helped with the mess inside the train and decided to go on to Abilene to get doctored up ourselves. We got Ribeye and the other two bodies on board, reloaded our horses, and Curly ordered the conductor to get us moving.

We were standing on the back deck of the caboose having a drink with the conductor as the train chugged on up that long uphill track and headed west.

Maybe half a mile behind us, two men on horseback come out of the trees on both sides of the tracks and met at the holdup site. They watched us for a few minutes and then rode south.

I said, "That might be Squeak, except he was alone."

Pug said, "I meant to tell you there was a fourth bandit. Other side of the train, up forward, and holding a gun on the engineer and fireman. Might have been Lord Jim. I was trying to get a bead on him out the other side door when all hell broke loose on your side. And my aiming and shooting was somewhat impaired, so it was, by someone stamping on my trigger hand."

"Seems like something impaired your durn vision, too," Curly snorted. "No way you could say it was Lord Jim or not?"

"No sir. If it was him, he has growed a beard since I last saw him, but he was wearing a bowler, same as Lord Jim does."

Curly raised an eyebrow.

"Derby. I believe you Yanks call them derby hats."

In Abilene two medicos cut and sewed and plastered us up pretty good before we went and got plastered some more on our own. We collected a four-hundred-dollar bounty on the two dead bandits and learned that Ribeye had a Choctaw wife and a son up in the Territory. Me and Pug decided we would split our reward money with his widow, but Curly said no, "Hell no, we would not." Which is why come we took the whole four hundred dollars to her along with his remains. A rich man can decide stuff like that, 'specially if he is feared.

I tried to ration with him. I said, "Curly, there must be a reason Ribeye left that squaw. Could be she is not one bit tolerable. And his share would only be a hundred dollars, anyways."

Pug added, "She might be well off. Might not even need the money. What if she has taken up with some Choctaw buck?"

"Who could blame her if she did? And there still is the boy. No, we will give her the entire bounty. Think on it a while, and I expect you will both come to the same conclusion."

Which of course we did manage to choke it down, bitter pill that it was. What Curly come up with next made it easier to swallow.

Chapter Twenty-Four

Next morning me and Pug were at the hotel, having coffee and fry bread. We were talking about what we might have done with an extra hundred dollars each, which Curly was bound and determined to just give away to some Choctaw squaw we ain't even met. Outside a rain squall had turned all that dust to mud.

"A brand new yellow dress," I said. "Heck, I can see Emmalee in it. And one of them new fishing poles, with a reel. New hat for me, too."

Pug nodded. "Solid ideas, Brodie. They would work for me, too, did I have a woman. And new boots. These is falling apart. But maybe a green dress, instead of yellow."

Curly came in just then, stamping his boots to knock the mud off. He yelled for a coffee mug and bit off some of my fry bread.

"You two clear your heads of them shawls and sewing machines you was gonna buy for your various ladies, and listen up. I have arrived at a long-term plan for us. Good one, too."

"Wasn't no dinky shawl, thank you. I was thinking of a really nice dress. Yellow." Truth be told, now, inside I was thinking that a sewing machine really would be a good gift.

"Green one," Pug said. "Dress, that is."

Curly squinted at Pug. "For who, exactly?"

"Maybe that widow Boyte, over to Weatherford."

"Good," said Curly. "She is part of the plan. Listen and learn, girls. Pug, you are not coming to the Red River camp with us, not right off. You need to take the train back to Weatherford, find that widow, and marry her. You'll be set for life, like me. Not just another dog-ass poor Ranger, like Brodie here. You with me so far?"

We just stared at him.

"All right, then. Soon as you can, you get the widow to sell that big patch of red clay to Brodie here. Get him a fair price. You know, maybe a dollar an acre."

I said, "Hold on here, Curly. Where exactly do I come up with . . . what, five hundred dollars? I mean, we got some cash, but nothing like that much. And we're saving to get enough for our own spread."

Pug was still staring at him, mouth open.

Curly smiled and said, "Calm down. I'll be your banker. Loan it to you, long term and low interest. Why would you want it, you might ask? Easy. To sell clay to Billy, is why."

He sat there grinning, as if he was making perfect sense.

"Curly," I said, "you are not making perfect sense. Why would Billy buy clay from me?"

"To make bricks, you idjit. In his brick factory. He'll need lots of red clay."

"What doggone factory?"

"The one I'm gonna loan him money to build. Me and Billy been talking, and he has some ideas on how to improve on how they's making bricks everywhere now. He studied on it at college. Just needs a little capital."

"And red clay," Pug said. "And a place for his factory."

"He could build on my land, but he says it makes better sense to put the factory near the clay, which happens to be closer to Dallas and Fort Worth."

"Which is where he'll sell a mess of bricks," I said, shaking my head as it came clear. "You been thinking on this awhile, you old bugger."

"I surely have," Curly said. "And he won't just be selling bricks local. If we was to run a rail spur in there, our bricks would ship all over."

"Lord, love a duck," Pug sort of whispered, as it sank in. "You keep saying 'we' and 'us' and 'our.' You're talking about a sort of partnership, are ye not?"

"That I am. Wade has been telling me that me and the missus need to diversify. Says bad weather or tick fever or whatever could wipe out the beef business, any given year. Says, on the other hand, folks is gonna keep coming west, having babies, and building homes. Says one taste of tornadoes or sleeping in a dugout or a doggone range fire, and they will all be wanting bricks."

"Judas H. Priest," I said. "So, you loan me and Billy enough to buy the clay and build the plant. You and your missus kick back and draw our payback for dang ever."

Pug said, "I get paid for the land, which is fine, but how about I borry enough to build that rail spur? It will cross my land." He laughed suddenly. "I sound like I'm already married, and I've yet to kiss her."

Curly said, "Now you're thinking. A rail line could move lumber, cattle, and people just as well as bricks."

"What about my boy, Wade? Where would he fit in?"

"Heck fire, Brodie, he'll be our lawyer. We'll all be paying him. And I'd expect you and Pug to give up on your high-paying Ranger jobs to be our foremen and run security."

"Give up fifty a month and sleeping on the ground? You have to let me think on that, Mister Sentell." Pug was smiling from ear to ear. "All right, I've given it careful thought, and I'm in."

Curly said, "Quit yapping and catch that east-bound train. Woo the widow. We need that clay."

"Yessir, Boss. And, faith, can you tell me what one of those sewing machines sells for?"

We heard the whistle of the inbound train, and Pug rushed out to catch it. Wasn't a minute passed before we heard this big hullabaloo from out on the porch.

Me and Curly stood, but, before we could take a step, a man came through the front door and jerked his thumb back over his shoulder.

"Fixing to start a little scrap out there. One of them gamblers is about to get his dandy bottom whupped."

"By who?" I said, as I picked up my rain slicker.

"Big feller who just came out. Arshman, I'd say, by the sound of him."

I said, "Oh, hell," as Curly pushed past me.

Outside, Pug had the little gambler by the front of his frock coat. Had him up there where his toes was barely touching ground.

"I said I was sorry, Boyo, even though it's unsartain who run into who. You call me another name, and I'll turn you over me knee and spank your drunken arse." Pug released him, and the man fell on his butt.

Curly grinned and said, "Don't you miss that train, standing around and bullying drunks."

Pug saluted and said, "On me merry way, Boss."

As Pug turned toward his horse, the gambler bounced up, pulled a knife, and ran at Pug's back. Curly drew his revolver and shot the man, while I fumbled with switching my slicker to my claw arm so's I could draw, too.

We were side-on to the gambler. Curly's .45 slug took him in the right shoulder and knocked him away and down. He dropped his knife but scrambled to grab it left handed. He went to stand up again, calling Curly a vile name.

The dandy should have stayed down and kept his mouth shut. All three of us shot him. With two .45s and my .44 slamming him from two directions, he jerked this way and that and then went face down in the mud.

As the smoke cleared, Curly growled, "I purely hate backstabbers. Hate 'em. I will simply not abide them."

Folks began to ease out. "You just had to kill him?" one said. "I mean, all three of you felt the need to shoot one little drunk?"

Chapter Twenty-Five

Curly squinted at the man. "And what's it to you, Abernathy?"

Lord Jim was obviously agitated and frustrated, but if he was scared of us it didn't show. He took off his derby and slapped his leg with it.

"He owed me a decent sum of money, Marshal Sentell. Has owed me for a good little while. He was coming to take me to his hiding place. His stash." Lord Jim held out both hands to his sides, palms up, and stared at the sky. "Really? You had to take him right now?"

"If I was you, I don't know as I'd speak to the Lord that-a-way," Curly said. "Could be he didn't recognize you, what with you shaving your whiskers and all."

That brought Lord Jim up short. He turned to stare at Curly. "Whiskers? What whiskers, for pity's sake? I haven't had a beard since I was twenty."

"You wasn't with Squeak a few days back? Delaying trains from their normal schedule? And don't call me no marshal. I put that behind me."

Jim said, "Well, Mister Sentell, that's just fine, but I don't have the first clue what you are speaking of. What trains?"

"Just one. The one from Weatherford to Abilene. The one we was on trying to catch up to Squeak. The one he held up, alongside a bearded man, looked like you, leastways to Ranger O'Hanley there."

Lord Jim turned to stare at Pug. "Really?" he said again.

"Something like you," Pug said. "Derby hat, but with a beard. I didn't say it was you. I said it could have been."

It started to rain again, sort of a drizzle. Lord Jim looked at heaven. For the third time he said, "Really?" Rain was running down his nose.

Curly still held a cocked Schofield revolver, still smoking, and now pointed at Lord Jim. So did Pug. I felt comfortable decocking my pistol, holstering it, and pulling on my slicker.

Lord Jim said, "May I come join you on that dry porch, Sentell? I was here all week. There are witnesses. You have just shot one of them to pieces."

Curly waved Jim up to the porch and said, "Get on that train, O'Hanley. Don't dally."

Lord Jim came on the porch and said, "When I last saw Squeak, he was in Fort Worth. With him were a drinking man and English Bob, a Scot actually, not so young and handsome as myself, but a bearded man who wears a bowler. I think the drunk was called Mule-Face, or something similarly stupid."

As Pug rode away toward the train station, I eased off the porch and went through the pockets of the dandy, as the rain pitter-pattered on my slicker and his dead back. Found twenty-seven in paper bills and a pouch of gold coins.

I handed the money to Lord Jim as I rejoined him and Curly on the porch. "Looks like maybe he went by his stash before he come to meet you."

Curly finally decocked his pistol and let it hang by his side. "Ain't that nice," he said. It wasn't a question.

"Yes," said Lord Jim. "Really."

A town deputy sauntered up about then. "I know some of you to be Rangers, so I'll take this to be justified." He spat in the mud and said, "Thing is, who's gonna pay for it?"

Curly said, "Pay for what, exactly?"

"Putting this here cheating piece of trash in the ground,

exactly. He ain't got no family nor friends to speak of. Sort of lived with a whore at the Red Dog Saloon. You think she'll pay? Hell, he probably owed her."

"Yeah, good luck with that," I said. "How much you figure?"

"Two, maybe three dollars, a coffin, and the digging. I guess I could fine his girlfriend, but that don't seem right. So who pays?"

Me and Curly turned to stare at Lord Jim then, but he didn't speak until Curly raised his bushy eyebrows and pushed his hat brim up with his pistol barrel.

"Very well, then," Lord Jim muttered. "I will give you two dollars, deputy. You can sell his stuff if you need more."

The hotel bartender had followed us onto the porch. He piped up right away and said, "I'll give you a dollar for them boots, Deputy Martinez. He wore the same size as me."

"A dollar a piece. Them are good boots. Quality. He was a dandy. Wore good stuff, and you know it."

"All right, all right, a dollar-fifty. They won't fit you, Martinez, and you know it."

Lord Jim handed the deputy two dollars. We left the two others to squabble and went back inside.

"And where might you be going next, Brodie?"

Lord Jim and Curly Jack was in the hotel dining room with me, having coffee. Trying to dry off some. Hoping the durn rain would quit.

Curly answered for me. "Depends on what more you can tell us about Squeak."

"I hope we're heading home," I said. "Maybe mend up some. But if you know exactly where Squeak was off to, I guess I'll tag along with Curly, even shot up and pitiful as I am."

"I can tell you very little more, actually," Lord Jim said. "Master Squeak said he was, and I quote, 'Going to put together a gang to go steal back some money that Sentell and the damned Rangers took.' He doesn't seem to understand that since he stole it from you, you actually have a claim on it. Rather, it's once his, always his, in his mind."

I said, "We didn't leave him much of a gang."

Lord Jim said, "There's one more thing that I think to be of real importance, most especially to you, Mister Sentell. Would you like to hear it?"

"Damn your eyes, Abernathy, spit it out," Curly nearly yelled. "Didn't nobody ever tell you that you got a knack for packing one sentence into a mere speech?"

"I apologize. Here it is, then: Squeak also believes you took that rich widow from him. I sincerely think he is convinced that he should be settled in as lord of the manor, rather than yourself. You might remember I once suggested to him we should take your money. And wife."

For once, Curly was speechless.

"Curly," I said, "that right there is a solid reason for us to go home and get well while we try to figure out what Squeak's going to pull next."

"You don't think that little bugger would actually hit my ranch? Try to take my stash and my wife?"

I shrugged. "Heck fire, Curly, if he thinks it's his woman and money already, that right there sort of proves he is bat-shit crazy. Don't it?"

Lord Jim said, "I agree with Brodie. Why not go home, watch for him, and put your Rangers on the alert for him?"

Curly said. "I take your point, Brodie. You, too, Abernathy. And what are your plans?"

"I was heading back to Fort Griffin. Perhaps I could ride along with you, that far. It's on your way."

Curly muttered, "Free country."

There was a loud crack of thunder, and the bottom fell out of that rainstorm. Lord Jim slapped his thighs with both hands, stood, and said, "Perhaps tomorrow, then."

Tomorrow turned out to be hot and steamy, with plenty of mud but clear skies. Curly had sent Ribeye's mortal remains on to his widow by train, along with a twenty-dollar bill and a note that I would soon follow with the rest of his money. And I thought he might of forgot. I said so, as the three of us headed northeast that sunny morning, by train to Albany.

"Well, Curly," I said, "I had hopes you might of forgot about paying off that widow."

Curly just snorted, but Lord Jim got the conversation started.

"Did you just say, 'might of?' I mean, not 'might have?' "

"He did," said Curly. "Heard it, clear as a bell. What of it?"

"I thought so. I have been straining for years to hear exactly what you were doing with that contraction, and you are substituting 'of' for 'have.' And by 'you' I mean most of you western colonials. Do you not realize what you are saying?"

Curly said, "Not saying about what, exactly?"

"What's a contraction?" I added.

"It is a combination of two words. You are saying, for example, 'would of,' when you mean to say, 'would've,' which is the contraction of 'would have.' Do you see?"

Curly turned in his seat to glare at Lord Jim. "See what? You just said that we say 'would of' when we mean to say 'would of.' Didn't he, Brodie?"

"I believe he did. Are you still drunk, Lord Jim?"

"No, no, no," Abernathy said. "I know they sound alike, but 'would of' and 'would've' are entirely different. And it's much more than that. You also say 'must of,' and 'couldn't of' when you mean to say 'must've' and 'couldn't have.' I mean, 'couldn't've.' I mean, no, that would be a double contraction. I'm not certain about that one. It's all so much more clear if it's written, rather than merely sounded out."

"What it sounds like to me is so much high English gobbledygook, to me. Lemme ask you something, Brodie. Have we writ this here uppity gentleman many letters?"

"None, Curly, to my certain memory. Nary a single one."

"And yet he seems to understand what we say, don't he?"

"Sort of," I said. "Or maybe I should say, 'Sort have.' How 'bout it, Lord Jim?"

He said, "No, 'sort have' is wrong. But I am able to tell exactly what you mean, even though you say it wrong."

Curly slapped away a horsefly. "Good," he smiled. "Enough said. You understand, Brodie?"

"Kind of. I ain't sure."

Lord Jim jumped right on that. "See now, Brodie, there is another contraction. 'Ain't' is an abbreviation for 'am not.' Do you see?"

Curly said, "And what if I say you ain't making much headway with this talk?"

"That's different," Lord Jim said. "Then it is short for 'are not.' But, in general—"

Curly laughed. "In general it's whatever you say it is, ain't it? What about that?"

Lord Jim shook his head and laughed, too. "All right, all right, I see what you mean. In that particular case, you are asking, 'Is it not?' I can see how this becomes confusing."

Curly said, "I ain't confused one bit. Brodie?"

"I ain't ever been so confused."

"Well, there he means, 'have not,' and I know—"

"Aw, just shut up, Abernathy. Quit screwing up my young pardner, and quit ruining my life. Get back to us when you can speak American."

Chapter Twenty-Six

The army had pulled out of Fort Griffin and lowered the flag in 1881, better than eleven years back. One reason they left was that the railroad chose to go through Albany instead of Fort Griffin.

We unloaded ourselves and our mounts in Albany and rode on northeast to what was left of the fort, a hardscrabble community called The Flat. We said goodbye to Lord Jim there.

"I hope this ain't your dream of a place to spend your olden days, Abernathy." Curly looked around and then spat in the general direction of the saloon.

Lord Jim gave Curly a nervous laugh and said, "I assure you it is not. I hope to collect a few small debts, then pick up the old Butterfield Stage Road and ride into Jacksboro. I wish you all safe passage home."

Curly started away, then turned back.

"You hear anything on Squeak, you find a telephone or telegraph and get me word straight away. You actually lay eyes on him, shoot him. Try to wing him and save him for me, but kill him if you have to."

With that, Curly lashed his horse, and we rode north.

Next day we were home. Curly pulled Segundo aside and said, "Have some of your vaqueros ride slow circles around the hacienda, like we was a nervous herd of steers."

The foreman said, "*Si, Jefe.* How long?"

"I ain't sure, Segundo. Maybe 'til we figure out where Squeak is."

"Ah, *si, Jefe.* Squeak. *Un poco cabron.*"

Squeak weren't nowhere to be found, for certain. Curly got the wires humming with every Ranger camp in Texas, and we got several possibilities, but the most likely was near San Angelo. A squirt, a bearded man, and a Mex had tried to rob a bank there, then shot and robbed a tinker south of town. He'd played dead and heard them say something about Del Rio.

"Sorry little bugger," Curly said. "Even messed up the murder of an unarmed tinker. They'll cross the border at Del Rio. I'll ask the Rangers and local law to watch for them there and down at Eagle Pass, maybe catch 'em coming back across the river."

I said, "They could cross that durn Rio Grande anywhere."

Curly shrugged. "Who don't know that? It ain't like we can seal that border. Heck fire, we ain't even sure this is Squeak's gang. You come up with a better idea let me know. Right now I need to give my vaqueros some rest."

Pug called, all aflitter, to say Rebekah Boyte had accepted his proposal. He went on to try and tell us about wedding plans, but Miz Sentell stepped in and took over. She had picked up on the drawing room phone.

"Put Miz Boyte on the telephone, Pug. I am thrilled with your good news and heartily congratulate you, but she and I will handle the planning."

Pug started to say something else, but Curly cut in and said, "Just say, 'Yes ma'am,' Pug, and save your breath. You'll be told when to dress up and show up, same as me and Brodie."

That wedding was the dangdest shindig I'd ever been to, up to that point. It was held at Curly's ranch, of course, and he didn't spare one drop of expense. Well, leastways his missus didn't.

There was beef, naturally, but also lamb and a whole entire hog on a spit. Segundo and his family did all the cooking, 'cepting for cakes and pies. There was tamales, frijoles, rice, chilis, tomatoes, fry bread, sweet rolls, sopapillos, chalupas, carnitas, enchiladas, empanadas, stuffed peppers, and fried catfish with hush puppies. And a few beans and some liquor.

My favorite was the pork. Segundo's wife cut and squeezed about twenty oranges into the pig's belly once he was turned on his back. That juice soaked into the meat, and I ain't tasted anything better, before or since. Near about hurt myself. Even Pug ate some.

Speaking of Pug, things did go a little sideways at first. He showed up, all tense, the day before the wedding along with a dozen relatives of his bride-to-be. Me and Emmalee was already there, what with her helping Miz Sentell in the kitchen, and me helping Curly with the sauce, so to speak. He grabbed me and steered me to the barn before he even said hello to Miz Sentell and Curly.

"Brodie," he half stuttered, "I don't think I can do this. I mean, I can't . . . I ain't . . ."

"Pshaw," I said, grabbing his meaty shoulder, "you'll be fine. Everybody gets a little nervous before their wedding. Look how happy she is."

"Look at me, Brodie. I ain't a *little* nervous. And it ain't her. I mean, it *is* her. I'm crazy about her, but I've never been with no one like her, and I ain't never done something like this before. I don't think I'm doing this just to get the clay, but what if she thinks so? She gonna chuck me out as a greedy brute? Sweet Jaysus, Brodie, how do you know?"

It hit me right then that he was eat slam up with guilt and close to pulling the plug on the whole wedding. It also hit me that this was a lot more important than some red clay.

"Take the damn clay out of it, Pug. Set it aside. What if we didn't want or need it? Look me in the eye and tell me you wouldn't still take a bullet for her. I seen you with her. Go ahead. Tell me."

He blinked a few times and scrunched up his brow, then nodded. "Sure, and I would. Hell yes, I would, but—"

"No buts about it, big feller. You done answered your own question. Now go hug Miz Sentell and Emmalee afore Curly asks what we's yapping about."

Things was total normal after that, and you never seen a happier pair than them two, nor a couple so relaxed after just knowing one another for such a few weeks.

Emmalee squeezed my arm and said, "They are just glowing. The love just beams off them. They remind me of us."

I said, "I seem to remember that you and me was acquainted quite some time before you acquired that particular glow. And some of his might be traced to that glass in his hand."

Should have just kept quiet, maybe smiled and nodded. She jabbed me in the ribs and muttered, *"Cabron!"*

I ain't certain I like her learning so much Mex. Anyways, it was a happy affair, and Curly promised the bride there'd soon be rail service from her home to his. He hugged her and told her and her kids they was always welcome at LT Ranch.

What followed was our long period of prosperity and growth. It wasn't like it was totally free of danger and excitement, but we all came through it in pretty good shape.

By the mid-1890s, you couldn't hardly believe the changes way out here on the frontier. There was telephones and trains everywhere, and even a few automobiles. Wade had passed the bar exam and was building up a fair practice. Billy had finished his studies at A and M and was all fired up over firing bricks. His talking kept on getting better, too. Listening to him, it was hard to believe he was the same "Cracked-head Billy" as was kicked in the skull by an ornery mule, maybe sixteen years back.

Over coffee in my kitchen, he said, "I've been to the three largest and most productive brick factories in Texas, Uncle Brodie." Leastways, he didn't call me his daddy no more. "My drawn-up plans take the best of each, and I've come up with some equipment designs to speed up the processes."

Of course, I would always ask about his engineering ideas. He would try to explain them to me, and I would try to understand and stay awake, all the while silently praying for a house fire or explosion or something, anything to let me escape. Cattle stampede, maybe?

"It's enough for me to realize that you know what you're doing, Billy. Please don't let me slow you down with all these details." Please. Pretty please.

"But here's the thing, Uncle Brodie. Wade is getting us patents on all this new equipment. Those other factories? They're gonna have to buy this stuff from us or pay us royalties, just to keep up."

Billy's factory was churning out wagonloads of bricks as more and more prosperous Texans wanted more sturdy homes. We couldn't hardly keep up with the orders. But Billy kept coming up with new doodads to make our stuff faster and better. And kept collecting royalties.

Once the rail spur was finished, we was shipping flatcar loads of bricks all over Texas, and some to New Mexico and Louisiana.

Some folks also wanted to ship stuff on the empty flatbeds as they headed back to the factory. We didn't own them, so we had no say-so on that.

We were talking about that over lunch in Weatherford. Me, Curly, Wade, and Billy.

Wade said, "We're making plenty enough to buy our own rolling stock. Pug told me he wants to do that."

I said, "If we owned our flat cars we could ship anything, anywheres. Right?"

"The way I see it, we needs an engine and cattle cars, too. And a Pullman car." Curly always thought big.

Billy had been doodling, but he woke right up for that. "A Pullman! Sure, for us to travel in. We could put a buckboard on a flat car, and our horses in a cattle car. We could go most anywhere, on our own schedule. I vote yes."

"You are talking an entire durn train here," I said. "Can we afford that?"

Curly said, "I don't know as we needs a caboose."

Wade said, "The real question is, can we afford not to? As for the cost, if we go together with Pug, we could buy two trains. I just don't think we need two. Not yet."

Curly said, "Talk to Pug, and get it started."

We got our first train. Our business really picked up after that, and then the war with Spain over Cuba started. Guess who got to ship horses and men and wagons and equipment to them Gulf Coast ports, to sail to Cuba? And we sold and shipped them a bunch of beeves, too, to feed the army and navy while they waited to sail.

We done right well.

Chapter Twenty-Seven

Evolved, he said. I heard him say it, plain as the nose on your face.

"Evolved?" I asked it politely. Wasn't no sarcasm nor sharpness in my question.

"Turned out," he said. "It means how things turned out."

Me and Curly Jack were finishing off a late breakfast at the Weatherford Hotel.

"Ain't no need for you to go all high and mighty on me, just 'cause you made it to that college and I didn't." All right, I admit I might have been a tad bit snappy with that one. "And you got bean sauce in your mustache."

Curly carefully wiped his mustache with his big, red, plaid bandanna, then pushed back and gave me his evil eye. Fired up a cigar. Checked his bandanna to see if any bean sauce showed.

"What kind of scorpion done crawled up your butt, Deputy Dent?"

I had just took a big bite of steak and couldn't answer him right off. My chewing was total furious.

Seeing he had the bulge on me, argument-wise, he went on. "It ain't like I was a customer of Texas A and M, Brodie. It weren't no more than a visit. And you'd have been there, your own self, hadn't you been off chasing Squeak. You and Pug both."

I finally spit out the gristle. "Which you had sent us to do. And I ain't your deputy no more. And 'customer' is wrong, anyways. You mean to say 'student.' 'Customer' ain't right."

"Now who is throwing around three-dollar words? You feel better?"

I didn't. "No, I ain't even sure what we was arguing about." I wiped my mouth and slugged down some fresh poured coffee. Thanked the waitress.

"We wasn't arguing, Brodie. I was just explaining that it seems to me that things has turned out pretty much how I seen it in my mind's eye, all them years back. You remember that conversation? Right here in Weatherford?"

"I do. Only it was in Abilene. We had just took the train from here to there. Seems like I remember better than you, which is a big surprise, seeing as how you tell me all the durn time just how smart you are."

Curly snorted. "I don't tell it no more than you talk about your blessed dream. You still have it? Wolves and a water hole and a little boy? No gun?"

"Rarely," I said. "But I don't ever forget it. It's still scary. Anyways, I know you was right about how things has gone. For all of us. The Sentell Brick Company. Made us all rich, and less than eight years in the making. Do you still worry about Squeak?"

"I do," he said. He twisted that big mustache of his, now gone completely white. "Word is, he's been in a Mex prison most of this time. But you know that."

"Yessir," I said, "but I'd surely like to hear that he'd passed on. Feels like I can't truly enjoy all this the brick company has provided us, what with looking back over my shoulder for that murderous little bugger all the time."

"Brodie, I just had a brainstorm. We'll send someone to Mexico to search him out. See is he still alive, and what his prospects are. Split the cost."

"You and me?"

"And Wade and Pug. We all got a stake in this."

"You want me to let Wade and Pug know?"

"I surely do," he said. "And I'm gonna ask Lord Jim if he'll take the contract to find Squeak."

I said, "How much you think it will cost us?"

He grinned. "Who cares, Brodie? We're all rich."

"Yeah," I said. "We've evolved pretty good."

"Well?"

I said, "Well, what?"

"Well, why'd you invite me to breakfast? It ain't like you to be overly sociable."

"Shoot fire, Curly, it escaped my thinking there for a minute. I wanted to talk about our hardware."

"Brick-making hardware, or guns?"

"Guns, Curly. I think it's about time to upgrade our arsenals."

"I'm listening."

"We need to talk about these smokeless powder cartridges some army units is using."

He said, "Only some?"

"Yessir," I said. "Many still has Trapdoor Springfields, but some has these new Krag carbines and rifles that use the .30-40 Krag cartridge. Army calls it the .30 government round. It's smokeless. And Winchester's new Model 1895 uses the same cartridge."

"Well, I can surely see it would be nice, not having all that white smoke marking your position, was you in a fight. And not have it blind you. One of the Rangers let me shoot his Model '94 Winchester .30-30. It's smokeless, too. Says it's a lot easier to clean up."

"Yeah, but there's more to it, Curly. This smokeless stuff burns faster than black powder. Pushes the bullet faster. And farther. And flatter. And they can use pointy-nose bullets that moves even faster."

"You can't use pointy-nose bullets in a tube magazine. One of 'em is likely to punch the primer of the one in front of it, set it off, and start a sort of a chainfire. The whole magazine is gonna blow up then, ruin the durn gun."

"These Krags and Model '95s don't have no tube magazines, Curly. They got box magazines, so the cartridges lay on top of one another. No chance of a chainfire."

"Back up some. How many rounds do they hold, and how much faster do the bullets run? They has got to be a tradeoff. And how do you know?"

I said, "They only hold maybe five rounds, but they shoot about five or six hundred feet per second faster than your Winchester. Maybe more. And the bullets don't weigh as much, by half. Some artillery professor in England has been studying on this since the end of the war, back in 1865."

He snorted like he always did when he weren't nearly convinced of my wisdom.

"Brodie, it ain't like we was a pair of dog-ass riflemen, worrying on how to tote forty rounds of rifle cartridges instead of twenty. And, as much as I admire a speedy bullet, I dislike giving up seven or more rounds in my magazine. We'll call Weakly's Store down in Brownswood. He's been ordering guns since 1875. He'll tell us what we want."

We called Old Man Weakley. His son-in-law Watson took the call, but I listened in, and he surely knew his stuff. After hearing all we had to say, he told us what we needed. Almost.

"Marshal Sentell, that fifty caliber model '86 is a fine gun, but with a slow, fat cartridge. Trajectory looks like a durn rainbow. This new .30-40 Krag round will boost your velocity from about fourteen hundred feet per second to about two thousand feet per second. Flatten that trajectory right out. Questions?"

Curly said, "Yeah, but how hard does it hit?"

"Hard to believe, but the same as your bigger slug." Watson went on. "Stopping power is measured as pounds of energy, and both cartridges deliver right at the same amount, simply because the new round is moving so much faster. So you can hit something or somebody much farther away and still have good knock-down power. Now, Mister Dent, your injury makes you favor the slide-action Colt Lightning. Makes perfect sense to me, but I can't get you one with a smokeless action. Colt don't make one. I can get you a Lightning in .38-55. It's black powder, but it's a bunch better than your .44-40."

"Well, it don't matter. I'm set on smokeless and high velocity. I'll take a model '94 Winchester carbine in .30-30. Marshal Sentell got to use one a while back and seemed to recommend it."

"You don't want a rifle? More beans in the tube? A slightly faster bullet?"

"I still spend a good deal of time on horseback, so I'm looking for a short saddle gun. I'll take a carbine."

"Well, it ain't like you're riding the plains, scrapping with a mess of Comanches on horseback no more and needing a mess of rounds in your gun. This .30-30 cartridge hits a lot harder than your .44-40, but the .30-40 Krag round is even more powerful. Let me order you both some Model '95 carbines in .30-40. You'll give up some rounds in your magazine, but you can top these ones off, just like the guns you carry now. And you can carry a bunch more of the new ammo, than what you're hauling now. I think it's the right thing."

We was quiet, so he went on.

"On your sidearms, there ain't no companion guns for these long guns. Best I can come up with is some new Smith and Wesson Frontier Double-Actions that will handle .44-40 smokeless loads. They are considerably hotter than the black powder

Schofield and Winchester rounds you're using now. Easier to clean, don't seize up none from that greasy black powder, and you ain't straining to see your target after the first shot. Break-tops, fast loaders like you got now. I got two left with five-inch barrels; you want a different length, I'll have to order it."

Curly said, "They don't come in .45 caliber? Smokeless, I mean?"

"No sir," Watson said, "but think on this. The .44-40 uses the same amount of powder as the .45 to push a slightly smaller slug, so it has more juice. It's why Winchester has always chambered their rifles and carbines in it instead of the .45 Colt cartridge."

Me and Curly looked at each other and realized we didn't have any questions. We gave him the order, and he said he'd call soon as the guns came in.

"One more thing," he said. "I ain't been able to get no .44-40 smokeless cartridges as yet. Demand is such that they is a one-month backorder delay on them. And when a factory says that, you can count on a two-month holdup. I'll keep on 'em about it and get you some fast as I can."

Two weeks later we got good and bad news all on the same day. On the upside, our new guns and some ammo was in. The bad news was that I might need mine.

Chapter Twenty-Eight

"Pop, a man called Teddy Roosevelt is coming to San Antonio to help raise a regiment of cavalry for Cuba. He was a bigwig in the navy department, but he resigned and took a lieutenant colonel's rank to fight over there."

Me and Wade were at our railhead, watching another trainload of horses head off east. This must have been early May of '98. Curly was with us.

Curly said, "I heard about him. He's the number two man, the segundo, under Colonel Leonard Wood. He's calling the outfit the 'Rough Riders.' Pulling in men from all over the West. Doctors, lawyers, lawmen, cowpunchers, circus clowns, you name it."

"Lawyers?" I said. A chill run down my spine. "What's your point, Son?"

"I'm gonna join, Pop. I've given it plenty of thought. No way you can stop me, but I really hope you can help me deal with Mama Em."

"She don't know yet?"

"No, sir. I wanted to tell you first. You and Curly, that is."

I couldn't get words out right away, so Curly stepped in. "I admire your gumption, Wade. I wanted to go myself. Sent 'em a wire and tried to volunteer my services. They said I was too durn old."

That stunned me, too, but I got over being speechless and said, "You want to know how to handle this with your mama?

You don't. You catch the next train to San Antone, let her find out after you're gone."

"I can't do that, Pop. I have to face her and kiss her goodbye. You know I do."

I looked at Curly.

"Don't look at me, Brodie. She's your wife. But I will say this, Wade. You got no idea what the army is like, most specially when it's being put together. Tentage, guns, ammo, rations for you and your durn horse, sickness, dumb-ass junior officers, drunk colonels . . . you name it—it'll be messed up. Now, was you to sign up as a lawyer, things would be a sight better. That I could see. A headquarters type. Even Brodie here could sell that to Miss Emmalee."

"I'm not going in as a lawyer, Uncle Jack. I'm gonna fight as a Rough Rider."

Curly said, "Awright, awright then. I understand. I was the same way, and your pop was too."

"I never was in no army," I sputtered.

"No, but you was a shot-up Texas Ranger when I met you, and you was younger than Wade is now. We had our wars. Let him have his."

"Thanks, Uncle Jack. I'm glad you understand."

"Me and your daddy understanding is one thing, but your mama is something else entirely. Her, you got to lie to. Right, Brodie?"

I caught on. "It's the only way, Son. You tell her you're going in as a lawyer. A desk job, nowhere near no fighting. It might work."

Wade looked dubious. "But lie to her?"

"Yes, indeed," said Curly.

"Like a sleepy dog," I said.

"It might work, if you back him up good." Now, Curly might

have said that, but he durn sure did not sound like he believed it.

Anyhow, I did back Wade up. Just not exactly how I planned.

See, my plan was to tell Emmalee I'd go with Wade to San Antone to get him safely into some desk job in the Rough Riders. And then to even go with him, if she really pushed it. Not that I had to worry about being allowed to go, what with my age and hook and all.

It started that way. Curly even come up with the idea to donate sixteen saddle-broke horses to the regiment, and to have me and Wade accompany the two cattle cars it would take to get them there. Figured that would get Wade off on the right foot.

Curly even made some calls. Told folks he was an old friend of Governor Sul Ross, which he was. And since Sul Ross had only died about a year earlier and was no doubt the most highly thought-of Texan anywheres just then, some skids got some serious grease.

Emmalee even bought it. It weren't exactly without tears or some shouting, but Wade proved he could lie as good as the next lawyer, and, by the time Curly had lined up the ponies and rail cars, my bride did come around. Me and Wade was rolling south the next day, with me steady trying to convince him to take a desk job whenever we got there.

"For my sake, Son, if not for your'n. Your mama will kill me."

"You had your chance, Pop. Let me have mine." And he'd smile. Wouldn't budge. I wondered how many fathers had gone through this same dance.

On the one hand I was proud, and on the other was fear. Worry he'd get shot or sick, and fear of Emmalee. I prayed somebody would call off this mess before it went too far, but the dang Spaniards had blown up the battleship *Maine* in

Havana harbor back in February, killing over two hundred sailors. After we declared war on the first day of May, most folks figured we'd be in a shooting scrape by the summer.

We finally dozed off somewheres north of Waco. I know that 'cause Wade woke me up somewheres south of Waco at a wood and water stop. It was still dark.

"Pop," he said, and he was right urgent. "Wake up. The horse cars are gone."

I can tell you for certain that ain't no way to come out of a sweet dream. If you was to guess I was befuddled, you would be far from wrong.

"Gone? Where? Where are they? Heckfire, where are we?"

"Easy, Pop. We're stopped for water outside of Austin. Conductor says our horse cars was dropped off back in Temple with some cattle cars. Thinks they was being shipped east. He says it was a mistake."

"Well, who don't know that? He better be glad it's me and you here, instead of Curly."

"Yessir, he's sorry as all get-out. There's no wire here, so I guess we get off in Austin and try to run 'em down by phone."

"Well, it ain't no good like it is. Guess you're right."

Two days later we finally got hooked up with our horses and rolled into San Antonio the next day. It was May 16th, 1898. As screwed up as that had been, things went downhill from there.

The regimental quartermaster was a captain, I think. He was right happy with our gift of horses.

"I want to introduce you to our executive officer, Lieutenant Colonel Roosevelt. He got in from Washington yesterday. You know who he is?"

"Big muckety-muck in the navy department," I said. "They got colonels in the navy now?"

He smiled. "No, sir, they don't. Roosevelt resigned and got a commission with us."

"Us?"

"First United States Volunteer Cavalry. That's his tent. Y'all wait here."

A few seconds later we heard someone say, "Bully!" from the tent. It was Roosevelt. Turned out he said that a lot when he was pleased.

He come bouncing out, wearing some lightweight, tan uniform and a monocle.

"Texas horsemen, eh? With Texas ponies. Jolly good! True patriots. I thank you for the entire country." He pumped our hands. "The damned Spanish upstarts don't have a prayer against this sort of true American patriotism, eh? Do they? No, of course not. I just pray we get there before they panic, surrender, and go home. No, sir, we want to give them a whipping." He slapped his leg with his riding crop. "So they don't try this again, eh? Will you join us?"

Wade said right off, "Yessir, that's the reason why I came. The mounts were my pop's idea. His." He pointed to me.

Roosevelt squinted at me. "And what sort of position were you hoping for, with such a generous gift? For your son, I mean. A captaincy, perhaps? What are his bona fides, sir?"

I sort of stuttered. I ain't seen nobody like him, before or since. "Well, he's a lawyer, and his mama . . ."

Wade cut me off. "I'm here to be a trooper, Colonel. I don't care what my mother wants. I have no military experience, and I'm no lawman. Like my pop is. Was."

"Bully. Bully for you." He clapped Wade on the shoulder, then turned back to me. "And you, sir. An old Ranger, I'll warrant?"

I nodded. "And marshal. I just—"

"Very proud. Proud indeed, both of you. With your prosthetic, though, my hands are tied, so to speak. I cannot enlist you, even as a trooper. Others like you have bravely tried."

I was still nodding. "Well, I want to—"

"Of course you do. Go with your boy. And you an experienced fighter and horseman. Not fair, not fair at all." He stopped suddenly and pushed his finger against my chest.

"Wait, now," he said. "By Jove, I may have the answer. What sort of pay do you require?"

"Pay? I don't—"

Wade butted in again. "He's rich. He doesn't need to be paid."

"Perfect! Mister Dent, you'll be my civilian hostler. No uniform, your own guns, of course, but you can certainly go with us. And we'll feed you. I'll work on the pay thing. Quartermaster, let it be done. And now I'm off."

And that's how I got to go to Cuba, or "Coober," as the colonel called it. I really didn't want to go home and face Emmalee anyway, not without Wade.

Chapter Twenty-Nine

I could write another whole book about our "Splendid Little War," as Colonel Roosevelt called it, but I don't think I will. It's enough to say that Curly was dead-on right about the build-up and move to Cuba being a total disaster.

Supplies and food and ammo was all over the map. Boats and trains didn't show up at the right place or time, and sometimes not at all. Some showed but left half empty. From San Antone to Tampa to Cuba, I ran in circles behind the colonel as he put out one fire after the other.

He did manage to get the Rough Riders issued Model '94 Krag-Jorgensen bolt-action carbines with smokeless ammo, which put us up even with the regular army cavalry units and the Spaniards. As we watched the boys drawing their new guns, he popped his riding crop against his leg, then tapped my shoulder with it.

"Dent, I am terribly glad we won't have to fight with single-shot Trapdoors and black powder, like our National Guard forces. Terribly glad. Those skulking Spaniards all have bolt-action Mausers. Seven-millimeter smokeless cartridges. Real zippers, I hear. Wizard rifles, those Mausers. But we shall prevail, never fear." He always talked like that.

What the Rough Riders did not have was rides. For lack of transport ships, four of our twelve companies was left in Tampa, alongside our horses and mules. All 1,284 of them, except two for the colonel. And one of them was lost in our landing.

All of a sudden, we was infantry. Wade called us the Rough Walkers, but for a while we was the Rough Sailors. From June 13 to June 22, 1898, we was aboard ship. But then we was going ashore, somewhere near Daiquiri and Siboney, Cuba.

It went about as smooth as everything else we had done, except hotter and wetter. Leastways, none of us drowned. Leastways, not as far as I could tell.

Once ashore Colonel Roosevelt went off to get orders while we assembled. When he got back he called the officers together, and I noticed they most all had Model '95 Winchesters, same as me. Seems officers weren't authorized long guns, so they bought them. Same as me.

That weren't a problem, as the Winchesters used the same .30-40 cartridges as the Krags our troopers carried.

Colonel Rosey, as some had come to call him, gave us a good little speech.

"We will march against the hills surrounding Santiago, about ten miles from here, along two jungle roads. The Tenth U.S. Cavalry will march beside us. The hills are occupied and fortified, but we will deploy and drive the Spaniards down into the port. These two hills are called San Juan and Kettle.

"Once the enemy is driven into town, our navy will shell them into submission, while we contain them. We should hurry the men along, as we expect little resistance between here and the hill forts."

Well, there was some good news there and some questionable facts. The Tenth Cavalry was an all-Negro regular army unit led by white officers, mostly, and veterans of thirty years of Indian fighting. They had good guns like us but was on foot like us, too.

Those "jungle roads" was more like winding streams. And that "little resistance?" Not exactly.

★ ★ ★ ★ ★

We started busting jungle along the sides of our trail then, with us on the left and the Tenth Cav on the right.

We struggled along for about five miles. It was so dense and hot and humid we might as well have been in a swamp. A swamp with hills. Big hills.

Finally, we took a break. Me and Wade was with "L" company.

"Pop, would you look? Can you believe I did this?"

I saw right off what Wade had done. He must have reached into a nest to grab one snake and grabbed two. He was holding both heads together in his right hand, and their fat bodies was trying to twist around his arm.

I couldn't say right off whether they was poisonous or not, but I could see that his knife was on his right hip. There wasn't no way Wade could reach his knife left handed to maybe deal with one snake, nor no safe way for him to separate them.

Before you could blink, I drew and blew off one of the heads.

It was a great shot. Wasn't nobody in the line of fire, and it didn't touch Wade's hand. It did splatter some blood and bits in Wade's face, howsomever, and the gun smoke sort of choked him.

"Good Lord, Pop!" He was startled, of course.

"I know," I said. "It was a helluva shot. I'm right proud myself. Can you handle the other one?"

"Proud? You're proud? It is only *one* snake! I find and catch a two-headed snake, and you shoot one head off? Are you kidding me?" He tossed the snake into the bushes and stood there shaking his head. "That's a hundred dollars gone."

I could see he was upset. I was fixing to start calming him down when there was a zip and bang right together, and some leaves was clipped in between us.

"Sniper!" I yelled. "Get down!"

Wasn't no need. We was already down, along with most everyone else.

"Your damn pistol!" Wade yelled back.

I know what he was upset about, other than his former two-headed snake. Wasn't yet no smokeless powder rounds for my revolver, leastways none I'd been able to lay hands on. That fat puff of white smoke in the green jungle had marked our position and kicked off the Battle of Las Guasimas.

A few seconds after those first two shots, the whole jungle in front of us lit up with Mauser fire. If you was looking right at one you might see a muzzle flash, but there wasn't no smoke to mark their positions.

Turns out we had walked right up to their battle line, across our trail. Hadn't been for my pistol shot we would have strolled into the middle of their position, and there was more of them than us. They could have wrapped around us and maybe wiped us out.

It was bad enough as it was, leastways for Wade's company. Sergeant Fish was killed right off, and the company commander, Captain Capron, stood over him firing his rifle until he was shot down. Me and Wade and his company got up and charged them, but fourteen more was killed and maybe sixty wounded. Most of his company. And Wade was gone.

Somebody saw him jump in a rifle pit full of Spaniards and start bashing them with his carbine and firing his Colt. They was stabbing at him with bayonets, but the whole line of Spaniards fled into the jungle. They must have got orders to pull back. Anyhow, Wade chased them.

I didn't see none of that as I had stepped into the stump hole of an old rotted tree. Near broke my leg, and then I got creased on the side as I got back up.

Somebody yelled, "Brodie's hit bad!" and I yelled back, "No, I ain't!" Turns out they were talking about Major Brodie. He was the number three man in the Rough Riders, behind Colonel Wood and Lieutenant Colonel Roosevelt.

It surely caused some confusion, as right about then Colonel Wood decided to take over the right wing and sent Rosey from that side over to the left where we was. And Major Brodie was either bad hurt or not, depending on whether you was listening to him or me.

Colonel Roosevelt grabbed a carbine and ammo belt and led us into a charge, and the enemy broke and ran.

Anyhow, I heard they found ninety dead Spanish in the jungle, but I can't swear to it. If it had been ninety thousand it wouldn't have brought Wade back. He wasn't there among the dead. I searched and searched and even stayed there looking and yelling as the regiment moved on, but it was no use.

Chapter Thirty

I never found Wade's body. Finally, the Rough Riders moved on, and Rosey himself rode over to me.

"I'll have the burial parties keep searching for your son, Dent, but you need to move with the regiment. We will avenge him and these other brave boys, but if you linger here some rear echelon jackass may arrest you for desertion."

"They could try," I muttered.

He was holding his revolver. It was a Model 1892 Colt Navy, recovered from the battleship *Maine.* He leaned down and tapped me on the shoulder with it.

"Look at me and listen, Dent. You must redirect your fear to anger."

"I ain't afraid of nobody, Colonel, and it galls me that you might think I was."

"I think no such thing, Dent. I meant that you should channel your fear of losing your son into rage against these damned Spaniards. Let's go among them. Are you with me?"

I was. Everything changed, right then. I guess that's what is called leadership.

When we got to the line of hills, our target was Kettle Hill, on the right. The First and Tenth Cavalry units was beside us. Other regiments was squared off against San Juan Hill, off to our left. I could see blockhouses atop both hills.

We was all under fire from the Spanish trenches, and finally we got the go-ahead to charge. I don't know if somebody else ordered it or Rosey just took it upon hisself. I heard later it was the darkies from the Tenth Cavalry who kicked it off.

Anyways, suddenly we was running uphill with Rosey riding amongst us, waving and firing that Colt. I saw him shoot down one Spanish rifleman as we crossed into the trench, and I was the first gringo into the blockhouse. My Winchester was empty, so I slung it and went in with my pistol drawn.

Two wounded Spaniards was the only things moving inside. They tried to raise their rifles, but I yelled at them and dropped them both with one shot each, and those .44-40 rounds nailed them to the floor.

There was several more dead Spaniards piled in a corner. The two on top was clearly dead, as they had the grey color of somebody who has bled out. I covered them with the Smith and Wesson and used my hook to unstack them in case somebody was hiding in the jumble. There was, and he gave me the shock of my life.

"About time," he said. "Lord, Pop, I thought you'd never get here."

I don't know as I've ever been speechless, but this time I come close. I finally stammered, "How the dickens did these two get killed and you not get shot, too?"

"They was my guards, Pop. They thought I was an officer when they captured me because I had a pistol and spoke Spanish. They were told to kill me as the others pulled out, but I grabbed a bayonet and did them both first. Pulled them on top of me."

"Are you hit, Son? Are you all right?"

He showed me a tourniquet on his leg. "Not shot, Pop, but they stabbed me pretty good in that fight back in the jungle. Banged me on the head, too."

Rosey ran in just then, leading some more Rough Riders.

"We beat them, Dent, we drove them off! Wait a moment. By

God, is that your boy? A miracle, sir, a pure miracle. You are bleeding, too, Dent. Let's get you both to the medicos."

So, that's how we won the battles of Las Guasimas and Kettle Hill. I would say almost single handed, but that would just be another poor joke about my hook.

There was more fighting that day and the next, but me and Wade weren't part of it. Our Gatling guns did get into it and purely ruined the Spaniards and drove them into Santiago, where our navy shelled them until they quit.

Colonel Roosevelt pulled every string there was to get Wade discharged and both of us on a fast boat to Tampa. "You both are entitled to medical care at government expense, Dent, but you are rich and will do better with your own doctors," he announced, in that pompous manner I had got right used to.

And he was right.

Chapter Thirty-One

With the war over, us in a new century, and all our prosperity, you might think Curly would slow right down and spend more time in a rocker on his front porch. I mean, he had Lord Jim watching the border, along with the entire Ranger force keeping a watchful eye out for Squeak. You'd think Curly might relax a bit.

Well, not so much. He owned thousands of acres by then and liked to keep his thumb on things, on and near the ranch. And my ranch, and Pug's. And the back forty. And Curly was always a force for good, as he saw it. A powerful force, too. Winchester finally brought out a smokeless version of the Model 1886, called the Fifty Express. Ninety-five grains of smokeless powder pushed its three hundred-grain fifty caliber slug at over two thousand feet per second. Of course, Curly bought one.

A new widow name of Constable had took up with a stove-up cowboy to help with her little hardscrabble ranch, just east of Curly's spread. Best I remembered, the man's name was Miller.

Whatever his name, he was a poor excuse for a man and turned out to be a terrible choice for the widow. Curly told me so himself. He showed up with no warning at my front porch, as I sat enjoying my first mug of coffee with Emmalee. In our rockers.

"Deputy, I need you to ride with me," he said.

Deputy, he said. He might just as well have said, "Goodbye, serenity."

"Well, good morning, Marshal," I said, big smile on my face. Big one. "Have you met my bride, Emmalee Dent?"

He turned red in the face and snatched off his hat.

"Well, shit," he said. "I mean, shoot. Good morning, Emmalee. You know how I am. I get on a mission, and my manners fly right out the nearest window. I do apologize."

Emmalee stood and gave him a smile to melt a rock. "No apology needed, Marshal. Not from such a dear friend."

"You are too easy on him," I said. "And you know as well as me, he ain't no marshal no longer. Not for years, he ain't been."

She looked at me with raised eyebrows. "It appears to me that today he is. I think you'd best saddle up. Will you step down and have some coffee, Marshal? He'll be ready in no time. I'll just go bag up some corn dodgers and cold chicken for your outing. How long will you two be gone?"

"Not more'n two days, Miss Emmalee. And might we have some cold biscuits and ham?"

We rode east on a cold morning, into the rising sun. Curly explained our "mission."

"Segundo followed about twenty head of our cattle onto the widow Constable's property," he said. "You know about the man she sort of hired?"

"Miller, maybe, but I ain't sure. He stole them?"

"Yeah, that's him, but no, I don't think he rustled me. Leastways, not yet."

"Why not?" I don't know why I couldn't just learn to keep my mouth shut.

"I'm about to tell you why, if you'll just shut up and let me finish. Segundo says our fence washed out along Cripple Creek, and them cattle just drifted, so we ain't going to hang nobody. Maybe. Anyways, not yet."

He stared at me, just daring me to ask another question. I bit my tongue.

"The problem is what he saw at the ranch house. He stopped by to tell 'em what he was doing, you know, recovering our stock. The widow and her two young'uns was on the front porch. Little girl and an even smaller boy. All three black and blue. All wrapped up in one blanket. You've noticed it's right nippy out?"

"They was beat up?" I couldn't hold back.

"Naw, they painted themselves, like durn Comanches. Of course they was beat up, Deputy. Why do you think we's heading that way? Miller was in the house, drunk. Segundo asked the widow if he could hook up her wagon and bring her and her kids back to my place, but she said Miller had sold the wagon for food and John Barleycorn."

"We taking a wagon?"

"Do you see ary wagon, Deputy? Nice of you to think of that, with your ranch miles behind us."

I didn't say a word. Lord, he was hard to handle when he was worked up. Took no prisoners whatsoever. I started to worry more for Miller than the widow and children.

"I sent Segundo thataway with a wagon this morning," he said. "Ought to get there soon after us. You think I'm stupid?"

I did not think any such thing. I was stupid not to think he would have took care of that. I just shook my head no.

It was twenty-five miles or so to the Constable spread. We rode most of it in silence. Finally I asked him, "Whatever happened to Constable, anyways? He just run off on her and the kids?"

"No sir, Deputy, I met him several times. He weren't the runner type. Hard working and loved his family to death. I stopped by once after he left. She said he rode south with a couple of men who was going to point him to a great deal on a bull and some cows. Even better price than I'd done give him. Took durn near all their savings."

"Curly, you know that ain't right."

"Clear enough to you and me. Back then, though, she was certain sure he was coming back."

"When was this?"

"Hell, Deputy, it's been over two years. Somebody murdered him for the money, or the cattle. Maybe his pony slid, fell on him, and their bones is mixed together down in one of these rocky arroyos. Anyways, he's gone."

"My point is, Curly, that was back before Squeak was last seen sniffing around these parts. Did the widow say that one of the men sounded English?"

"Lord, I never let that occur to me. I didn't ask, Deputy, and I should of. Could be where Squeak got his traveling money."

"Well, we don't know that and might never will. Main thing is that life can still be hard out here. Even harder for a woman with kids and no man. Probably why she took up with this Miller feller."

Chapter Thirty-Two

We got to the widow's spread by late afternoon. Nobody was in sight, but smoke was rising from the chimney, and there was two saddled horses tied up outside. One more was loose in the corral out back.

Curly pulled his long gun, swung down, and went up on the porch. I did the same.

"I hate to dismount uninvited," he said, in a low voice.

"How come we're doing it then?"

"It struck me that this butthead Miller might not ask us to step down. And don't it concern you that them two mounts at the rail right there might belong to the same men her husband rode off with?"

I hated to admit I hadn't thought of that, so I didn't say anything.

He said, "Anyways, I mean to go inside and check on her and her offspring, invited or otherwise."

That "otherwise" captured my attention. I checked the chamber on my carbine and left it on half cock. He banged on the door.

Some man yelled, "Who's out there?"

Curly yelled back, "It's Jack."

"Jack Slade? You old rascal, what brings you out here? Hang on, I'll get the door."

The door swung wide, and we stepped in. Curly cocked his carbine and said, "You Miller?"

"Well, yeah, but you ain't no Jack Slade." Miller seemed right drunk, and stupid. He wore his boots and long johns. Filthy, torn, and smelly long johns.

"Never said I was. I come to see Miz Constable. You just step back some. Deputy, cover them two."

Them two was the men sitting at the table with cards and a bottle between them. They wore gun belts but looked to be too drunk and startled to pull on us. The widow and her children sat on a rope bed against a side wall, opposite the fireplace. They were pitiful. I remembered her as a pretty young wife three years ago. Now she looked to be forty, all haggard and washed out. And bruised.

"These two the same men as rode off with your husband, Miz Constable?"

"That you, Mister Sentell?" She seemed to be all confused and scared.

"It is me. You'll be all right now, but answer me: is this them?"

"No sir," she muttered. "They was three of them, back then. One of them was a Mex, and another was maybe English. Little one with a high voice was the boss."

Miller backed up some more, and the two men tried to stand, both raising their hands. One said, "Jesus, Billy, that's Curly Jack Sentell."

The other said, "We didn't mean to do nothing to piss you off, Marshal. We'll just head on out now."

I motioned with the carbine for them to sit. Two did, but Miller stood there fidgeting.

"Damned if it don't seem Squeak has struck again, Curly. I mean, before he headed into Mexico."

"It appears you might be right, but I'll oblige you and them to watch your mouths in front of this young lady. Anyways, the family don't look no better than Segundo described them, do they?"

"Even worse than I expected, Marshal."

Curly said, "Miz Constable, I'm sorry to find you in such a sad condition. I fear I've been a bad neighbor. My wife has asked me several times to check on you, but I let poor excuses get in my way. Now, have you tooken this man Miller as a husband?"

"That ain't none of your business," Miller snapped. He maybe had not heard of Curly.

Curly pointed his Winchester at Miller's crotch and said, "I'll decide what's my business, boy. You might find it interesting that I hate a wife beater. I despise anyone who hurts children even worse, and these here little people didn't pick up them bruises falling down no short flight of steps like I seen outside."

He took a breath, then raised his barrel up to Miller's nose. "Now I'll thank you to keep your pie-hole shut while I talk with Miz Constable, husband or not."

Curly half turned to the widow and raised his bushy eyebrows.

"He ain't my husband," she barely whispered. "I took him on for help just 'cause he'd been hurt, and we was in need. The deal was to be I could feed him, but he done took over."

"You want him and these other yahoos gone from your ranch?"

She nodded.

Curly uncocked, then jabbed Miller in the belly with his gun barrel. When Miller doubled over, Curly slammed him in the side of his head with the butt, which floored him. Curly cocked the carbine again and pointed it at Miller's head.

He said, "You want me to shoot him?"

The saddle tramp went white faced.

"Go ahead," one of them said.

"He don't mean nothing to us," said the other.

"I weren't talking to either one of you idjits," Curly snarled. "I was talking to the widow."

She shook her head.

"Fine," said Curly. "I got a wagon to carry you and your family to my place. Be here any time now. Y'all can stay until you're better. These other two scoundrels—did they abuse you, too, or was it just Miller?"

She muttered, "Just Miller, so far."

He turned to the two men. "Ease them pistols down on the floor. Deputy, go get their long arms, and bring 'em in." He kicked Miller in the ribs, but he didn't even flinch. Out cold as a rock.

"Where are Miller's guns?" He spoke to the widow again, softly this time.

"Gone. Traded for likker, too," she mumbled.

Turning back to the two men, he said, "Y'all pull this slumbering piece of sh—, uh, dirt outside and ride. Right now."

"But he ain't got no horse ready to ride," one whined.

"I could shoot you, and he'd have one!" Curly shouted. "You don't warm to that idea, maybe you ride double with him."

"That'll work," the whiner said. They grabbed Miller's legs and started to drag him out.

The widow spoke up just then. "You're letting them scum-sucking pigs off mighty light."

Curly said, "What, these two?"

"All three," she said. "Miller was trying to sell both my children and my ranch to them two. They was haggling on a price when y'all busted in. I had done told him he'd sell my young 'uns over my dead body. He said that weren't no problem. I believe he meant to leave me dead on the prairie."

Curly pointed his Winchester at the two scoundrels. "Let him lay, right there. Close your eyes and hold your breath."

They were so drunk and stupid that they did just what he said.

Curly looked at me and nodded toward the smaller man,

then butt stroked the whiner right in the face. The whiner's mouth and nose gave out a solid crunch. He sat, pouring blood.

I didn't wish to damage my carbine, but I swung it and hit the other man in the forehead with the barrel. He bounced off the door and went down on his face. He didn't stir.

Curly had already begun to kick Miller in the head, but he glanced up at me and said, "The whiney one ain't finished, if you ain't all tired out."

I smiled and nodded. It was hard to get a line of credit with Curly, no matter how I tried. I swung the rifle against the side of Whiney's head, and he went over and lay still.

Curly kicked Miller two more times, then paused and looked at me. "Listen, I think you should go on and shoot those good old boys in the foot. I'd do it, but I fear my Big Fifty would take their feet clean off."

I said, "Both of 'em?"

"Both men," he said. "Not both feet."

"I really did get that much, Curly. I meant, just these two and not Miller?"

"Just these two. Miller's already crippled. See, I'm gonna let the three of 'em walk out of here, but I don't want it to be easy for them. Then we'll go and sell their horses and tack for Miz Constable."

He looked at her and said, "Think that'll be enough for what they done here?"

She just stared at him.

"Let's drag them outside first, Deputy. Spilt enough blood in here already."

We each grabbed an ankle and pulled the small one out, then rolled him off the porch. Went back in and did the same for the whiner.

As we started back for Miller, Curly stopped and put his meaty hand on my shoulder.

"Lemme just catch my breath, Deputy. This is tiresome work. Now, tell me true—do you reckon she feels like they're being punished enough?"

There were two blasts from inside.

"Maybe not," I said, as I followed him back in.

The widow stood over Miller's body, holding a Colt .45 discarded by one of the tramps. It was clear he hadn't switched to a smokeless model, as the room was slam full of gunsmoke. The little girl was screaming and holding her ears, and the boy rushed by us to get outside.

I said, "Sweet Jesus!"

Curly said, "I feared you weren't quite satisfied with the punishment, but you said you didn't want me to shoot him."

I don't think she could hear him. Probably deafened by them confined gun blasts. I said, "I believe she meant that she wanted to take care of that herself."

She said, "He didn't have no right" and shot him again, holding the revolver in both hands against the recoil.

Curly eased over and took the revolver from her, then passed it back to me while he comforted her. Her little girl grabbed her legs.

"You'll be all right, now. Probably better you did that, other than one of us. Let's get you and the sprouts cleaned up now. I believe I hear my wagon rolling up. Deputy, send the boy back in and finish up with them tramps."

I picked up the other loose pistol from the floor and started out. It was a little Lightning Double Action .38, which would do less damage than my .44s. To somebody's foot, for instance.

Curly said, "Afore you go, you might oughta make sure Mister Miller is total finished."

I looked. Mister Miller had a new eye in the middle of his forehead, along with a fresh puddle of blood growing him a bright-red halo.

"Total," I said and walked out.

Segundo was standing over the two unconscious cowpokes, loosely covering them with his shotgun. His oldest boy sat in the wagon.

"I brung blankets, Señor Dent. And some clothes, from my wife and muchachos."

"That's good, Segundo. Y'all take 'em on inside. I ain't through with these two."

I shot each one in the right foot, up near the toes. It woke them right up, even though it weren't but a pissant .38.

When they stopped hollering, I said, "Start walking, but leave your gunbelts. Vernon is thataway, or you can head south and jump a train. You'll cross water, either way. Don't come back."

The whiner said, "Can't we have one horse?"

"No, sir," I said. "Life is hard out here. Even harder when you're stupid."

As I walked back inside, Curly was handing Segundo's son the guns we took off them two drifters.

"You and your padre can have these, Tomaso. They's a pair of horses outside that need to be stripped, wiped down, and put in the corral. Make sure they got feed and water for a few days."

I handed Tomaso the gunbelts and that little .38, too. He nodded at Curly and me, but he weren't really paying no mind to anybody but the widow. She had cleaned up some and lost ten years of age. Not hard to look at, neither. And she was a widow. Who owned a ranch, outright.

As we headed back to Curly's ranch, I said, "You remember your missus telling you that you needed to carve out a spread for Segundo and his family?"

He said, "I do. What about it? Ain't no hurry, as I'm aware of."

I jerked my thumb back toward the wagon. "I think that problem has been took care of."

Chapter Thirty-Three

Next word of Squeak was a telegram from Lord Jim, down on the border. "He is leaving Mexico and is bent on revenge. Meet me in Weatherford?"

Curly agreed, and we caught the next train smoking.

In the hotel there, Lord Jim repeated his report.

"Revenge?" Curly scratched his bald noggin.

"Yeah," I added. "It's him as owes us, not the other way around."

Lord Jim shrugged. "It's what he said. I warned you of his backward thinking years ago. Remember? At any rate, I sent one man to Piedras Negras and another all the way to Ojinaga, while I waited in Ciudad Acuna. On that thought, I need fifty dollars each for those two men."

Curly said, "You want us to pay for two wild goose chases?"

Lord Jim said, "They were only wild because I ran into Squeak in Ciudad Acunas. He did not know I was working for you and still does not know. He said he'd been in two different prisons or jails and was trying to ascertain where best to recross the river. I told him that there were Rangers watching for him in Del Rio and Eagle Pass and suggested he cross at Ojinaga."

I said, "How come?"

"It is farthest from here, which gave me more time to warn you. And my man in Ojinaga confirmed he crossed there a week later. Yesterday, to be more precise."

Curly said, "Why didn't you shoot him?"

"I knew you would ask that," said Lord Jim. "He was on full alert and had two men. No opportunity availed itself. He was not even drinking, and, as soon as I told him Ojinaga was his best wager, he took his men and headed west."

Despite all the progress that came after the turn of the century, life in west Texas still had more than its share of rough edges. We hadn't had no word on Squeak's possible whereabouts for maybe a month, and then word came of a godawful crime spree a little east of Lubbock.

It had the stench of a Squeak operation.

"Robbery, rape, murder, and kidnapping," Curly said. "Minister and his family is the victims. Ranger sergeant called me on it, said he thought I might be interested. Said it might be Squeak." He took a sip of coffee. We was sitting in his kitchen, early of a morning.

"You called me to come to here ready to travel. I figured it might be him. Why come the Rangers think it's him, and who'd the bandits take?"

"I am coming to all that, Brodie, if you will stop interrupting me. They was a Mex handyman who hid in the barn and seen it all. Said the bandito boss was a skinny gringo with a high voice. He had two men. One was a saddle tramp, and the other wore a beard and a derby."

I got excited. "Sure sounds like them, Curly. Did he say the one sounded English?"

"There you go with the interruptions again. The witness was a Mex, Brodie. He don't know the difference between an English accent and American. We's all gringos to him. Now, where was I?"

I said, "You was telling me about the witness . . ."

"I know where I was, dammit. Listen and learn. The gang killed the preacher and his two boys, then raped and killed the wife, then took the daughter. She's maybe thirteen, fourteen."

"Thirteen," I said. "Jehoshaphat Christmas. But why go after a preacher's family? I ain't never known them to have much to steal."

"I had the same thought, Brodie. I was coming to that, before you cut in again. The Ranger said they was known to be raising money to build a new church and orphanage, and that's what put the bullseye on 'em. I say we head over there. See can we pick up their trail."

I stood up and said, "I hope you ain't waiting on me."

An hour later we was heading for a train, pulling a spare and loaded for bear.

"We have wasted a week on trains and trails, and rumors and wild geese, Brodie."

We was saddling up after another night in another friendly barn. I felt the same as him, but I'd had a nagging thought for a few days, and I said so.

"What if they is heading for your spread, Curly? That possibility has worried me some."

"Well, why in hell didn't you say so sooner? Let's ride. And don't keep all your bad thoughts to yourself."

I had several clever answers to that, but fear and common sense got the better of me.

"Yessir," I said.

Early morning three days later we was back in Curly's kitchen, wondering where everybody was. The phone rang. Curly answered it, then held it so's I could hear. It was Squeak.

"I got your lawyer here, Sentell. Young Mister Dent ain't hurt bad yet, but I need you to bring me that thousand dollars you took from me, and we'll trade."

Curly gave me a pained look, like to say he was sorry. I

signaled him with my fingers to go ahead, so he jumped right into the negotiations.

"It weren't but about eight hundred dollars we recovered. You had done spent or lost the rest."

"Well," Squeak shouted, "it's done gone back up to one thousand! That's the number, old man."

Curly muttered, "I got no wiggle room, do I? I'll bring it. Where to?"

"West end of the Copper Breaks Lake, where that trail from the ranch ends. You know it?"

"Yeah, I know it. I'll be there fast as I can, which I make to be late today. Does the boy need a horse?"

"They come in a wagon. I got no need for it. He can drive it right back home."

" 'They'? Who's 'they'?"

"Oh, yeah. I meant to tell you. I got your wife, too."

"My missus? You got my missus, too?" He stared at the phone, then looked at me.

I whispered, "Emmalee?" Please, I thought, please don't let him have her.

Curly finally got his voice back. "Anybody else?"

"Naw, Sentell, nobody else from your place."

Thank you, God. Thank you, thank you.

"How much for my wife? I'll pay whatever you want, whatever I got."

"Oh, no. She won't cost you nothing. Not one dime. I'll tell you why when you get here."

"She better not be damaged. Don't you hurt her. You hear me?!" It was Curly's turn to shout.

"Not to worry, old man. I ain't gonna hurt her. Fact is, I might keep her. That's why she won't cost nothing. Our English friend is watching her."

Curly didn't say anything. I guess he was stunned. I know I was.

Squeak went on. "I can hear them wheels just a-churning in your head, Sentell. I'll warn you once. You come alone and don't try nothing, or I'll shoot her first, then the boy. You know I'm desperate. I'll do it."

"I believe you. I seen what you did to that family over near Lubbock. You still got their little girl, or did you kill her, too?"

"I still got her. Now that I got your missus, I might let the Englishmen and the cow puncher have the girl."

"That's Brodie's boy you got, Squeak. You know I can't stop him from coming."

"He's with you? Bring him on. Just make sure he's right with you, not sneaking around off to one side or behind us."

Curly said, "Where you calling from?"

The line went dead.

After Curly stopped cussing and breaking things, we talked some more.

I said, "He didn't say nothing about hurting Emmalee, did he?"

"No, he did not, but where is she if he don't have her, too? You checked your house when we got back, right?"

"I did. Weren't no sign of her. I figured she was with your missus."

"Little bugger must of called us from Amarillo."

I said, "He could have tapped the line anywhere betwixt here and there."

"Well, leastways he ain't at the meeting place. Ain't no telephone lines nowhere near it. We move fast, maybe we beat 'em there."

We heard a buckboard pull up out front and walked out to find the big foreman, Segundo, helping Emmalee down. My heart jumped to see her, and I jumped to hug her.

Once we got caught up on what we knew, Emmalee told us how Miz Sentell and Wade come to be in Squeak's hands.

"A man came by and said he knew we were looking for clay deposits, especially gray clay. He said he'd come to take somebody to see the clay deposit, over near Copper Breaks. The thing was, though, that he insisted that he'd only negotiate with Mister or Missus Sentell, as the true owners of the company."

Curly said, "What was his name, Emmalee? And what did he look like?"

"He was English or maybe Scottish. Derby hat, and he had a beard."

"But not Lord Jim," I said. "You do remember him, right?"

"I do, Brodie. This man was not as handsome as Jim Abernathy, nor as well spoken. And no gold tooth."

"English Bob, sure as I'm setting here." Curly slapped the table, then jumped up. "Why on God's green earth would she go with him?"

Emmalee said, "Wade told the man he was your lawyer, and he would go, and said he could not see why your wife needed to go, too. The man insisted, and Mrs. Sentell said she'd go, because she knew how important the gray clay was. You know, for this big order of bricks. Non-red bricks, she said."

Segundo butted in right then. "Wasn't no stopping her, *Jefe*. *Muy importante,* she say. Señor Wade, he say it was, too. And he say it was not too far from here. I'm sorry, *Jefe*. I should have stopped her, or gone with them."

"You damn well should have, Segundo." Curly was hot and wouldn't let up. "I surely expected better of you."

Segundo nodded. "Anyways, Wade went with them, and it ain't but twenty miles. Maybe less."

I said, "Ease up, Curly. She probably told him to stay here."

"You don't tell me to ease up, Brodie. Don't none of you tell me what to do. Now, I ain't through fussing at you, Segundo, but this minute you go get two good mounts and a spare. Get me supplies for a week. And medicine."

"Medicine, *Jefe*?"

"Whatever we got. They's gonna be shooting, and people gonna get hurt, I guaran-damn-tee that. Hurry up, damn you."

Red faced, Segundo rushed off, shouting orders in Mex.

Curly stood there, staring off to the southwest, towards Copper Breaks Lake. It was just off one corner of his LT Ranch. We'd been there before, in Bull Canyon. I expect he was seeing it in his mind's eye. I know I was trying to.

"I know where they'll be," he said. "They's a ledge, halfway up that big hill overlooking the trailhead. They'll be set up there, or I'll eat your hat."

"All right," I said. "Good to know. I just don't know why you're grinning. If you're right, they'll have the bulge on us, for certain sure."

"Only we ain't going to the trailhead, Brodie. We'll circle wide behind 'em and go on the sneak, up to the top of that hill. You starting to catch on?"

"Yessir, I am. But what if they ain't where you think? What if they're on top?"

"They'll be where I say, Brodie. They's a good little path, one horse wide, from the trailhead right up to that overlook. Kind of flat spot behind some rocks to tie off their mounts."

I wanted him to be right, but I couldn't see what he saw. This was all too serious. *Muy, muy, mucho importante.*

"Well," I said, "what about Wade's wagon? It can't go up no one-horse path."

"Which is why they'll leave it at the trailhead. I've been there, with the missus. You ain't got a good view of the trailhead from the very top. The ledge is perfect. Trust me."

"All right," I said, but my heart was in my throat. And we

wasn't even there yet. Think how constricted I was going to be, once we were in pistol range, what with them holding Wade and Miz Sentell. Judas H. Priest.

Chapter Thirty-Four

Several things come up as we rode toward Copper Breaks Lake. First off was who to expect at the trailhead.

"Curly, did you understand Squeak to say 'Englishmen' when he was on the telephone, or did he say 'Englishman'? I took him to mean more than one."

"I been turning that over in my mind, Brodie. What I'm afraid of is that Lord Jim is in on this, too. I know you ain't been total trusting of him."

"Nor you ain't neither," I said. "I hope it ain't so, as I've mostly liked him. But I won't have no trouble dropping a hammer on him if he's there. Now tell me about that bullwhip tied on your saddle." That was the second thing.

"Do I take that little peckerwood Squeak alive, I mean to flay the skin off him before I kill him. Same goes for Abernathy."

I expect my durn eyelids touched my hairline. Even from an old hard case like Curly, that was a shock to me.

"Clear enough. Just how do you see this rescue going down? I mean, you ain't total set on taking Squeak alive, are you?"

"Not him, nor none of his cohorts. Don't dwell on it, Brodie. I just meant if he somehow survives. As to how we move on them, I ain't sure till I see the ground. They can see the trailhead and turn-around site from their ledge, but we can't."

"But we'll have a good view of their ledge? This place you're sure they'll be waiting at?"

"I'm sure. Just wait and see. Way I remember it, they is knee-high buffalo grass from the top where we'll be on down to their ledge. Which gives me a plan."

He snapped his fingers. I swear. I seen it. We was less than three miles from the lake, swinging wide north to come up behind it, and he come up with a plan.

I nearly choked. "You about to share it? Or maybe you want more time to work it out?"

"Here's how it will go, Deputy." I always became "Deputy Dent" when things got really tense. That by itself was a pretty good warning to me.

"I'll stand and surprise 'em, tell 'em to drop their irons or we'll kill 'em. You'll stand, too."

He was really trying to scare me, I guess. I said, "And what if they point them irons at your missus or my son? He swore on the telephone he'd kill them."

"Of course he did, and he means it. It's all part of the plan, Brodie. Soon as he threatens our people, we give up, throw down our guns and go down to 'em. Only we don't really disarm."

"We don't?"

"No, sir. Before I ever brace 'em, I'll tie my Winchester to my ankle with that bullwhip. Drag it down in that deep grass till we're close. Then I'll move ahead and put the carbine right beside you. When I go down, you grab it and start shooting."

"Go down? You mean wait 'til you're shot?"

"Naw, naw, naw, Brodie. I'll fake that I trip or something."

I felt some better. "What about you?"

"They'll make us shuck our belts and pistols. Ain't you still got that little Merwin Hulbert .38 in your saddle pockets?"

I nodded.

"Give it to me now, and I'll tuck it in my boot. And here. Take my little Remington two-shooter and stick it in your arm can like you did in Tascosa. In case it really goes bad. Which it won't."

"Who do I shoot first?"

He said, "No way to know that till we're close."

It was right then that I realized this was exactly what my dream was about.

"Lord have mercy, Curly. Do you remember my bad dream?"

"The one with the little boy and the wolves around the water hole? How could I forget, seeing as you don't go no more than six months without having it?"

"Yeah, that one. Don't you see this is what that dream has been all about?"

"Listen, Brodie. I don't need you losing your entire mind right now. This ain't nothing like your dream. Ain't no water hole, ain't no little boy, and we are well armed."

"Well," I said, "there is a lake. And maybe we're well armed until we start down that hill. Unless they start crying and throw down their guns and surrender. You see that happening? And you done clean forgot about the wolves in my dream."

"What you don't seem to grasp ahold of here, Brodie, is that the wolves is you and me."

We left our horses hobbled well back and climbed to the hilltop. It was pretty much how he described it.

The lake was there, sort of ahead and to our right front. The road from the ranch come in from the trees on the left and disappeared down to where the trailhead must be.

That was blocked from our vision by the ledge maybe fifty-sixty yards downhill from us. The ledge where they would be waiting on us. The empty ledge.

"Sweet Jesus, Curly. I mean, Sweet Jesus. They ain't here." I whispered, but it might have been heard in Fort Worth.

Curly was furiously tying his Winchester to his leg above his boot. "Don't panic, Brodie. It has to be here. And it just come to me they might make us shuck our boots. Now, they is a round in the chamber, and it's on half cock, but I'm locking the lever down so's it don't pull open as it's dragged. You'll need to unsnap it for your second shot. And we needs to cuss and bitch the whole way down, so as they don't hear my carbine pulling behind me."

I come to within an inch of shouting, "Quit fooling with your whip and your leg. They ain't here!"

Instead, clear as a chapel bell, I heard Lord Jim shout from way down below, "No good. I can see you. I have been able to see you, quite clearly, for two hundred yards."

Me and Curly ate dirt.

Chapter Thirty-Five

The next voice we heard was Squeak, yelling back at Lord Jim. "Well, shootfire. What do we do?"

Lord Jim shouted, "You'll have to proceed upward to that next ledge."

Over the next fifteen minutes, Squeak's gang slowly appeared with their horses and hostages, on the ledge right below us. Just like Curly said. Last one up was Lord Jim.

"Just like I told you, Deputy," he whispered and grinned. It was a frightening grin. "I just hate Lord Jim is in on it. I liked him. Hoped he'd be our inside man."

"Wipe the dirt off your mouth, Marshal."

He did. Once they took care of hobbling their horses he whispered, "No time like the present." He stood and yelled, "Drop your weapons, you miserable sons of bitches!"

I struggled to my feet, too, and tried to look fierce.

It took them by surprise, for maybe ten seconds. Then Squeak put a pistol to Miz Sentell's head, and English Bob put one against Wade's.

We froze, just like Curly planned.

"Drop them long guns, and your pistol belts, too!" Squeak yelled.

We did. That involved me coming out of my suspenders, which held my gun belt.

"Toss your vests and turn around. Best not have no hideaway guns tucked in on your backsides."

We did what he said.

"Now take off them boots and show them."

"Bugger," I said. Then, of course, it started to rain.

"Bugger, double bugger," I said.

"The rain is good. Hard on their eyes looking uphill at us," Curly whispered. "I'm tying your pistol to my ankle with the whip."

"What did you say?" That was Squeak.

Curly yelled, "I said, 'It'll be *good* and *hard* on our feet, walking down *hill*! Might break my *ankle* and *slip*!' Can't you hear nothing?"

"This ain't supposed to be no cake walk for you, old man. Not like when you shotgunned me from the back of that train. I took five buckshot and near died."

"Yeah, I guess it is more like when you shotgunned them women and children, down the side of that other train. Must have been a proud moment for you. Some of them did die."

Squeak cocked his pistol and shouted, "Somebody else is gonna die right soon, if you don't quit jawing and mosey on down here, pronto!"

I noticed Lord Jim give Squeak a harsh look but couldn't make nothing of it. Curly said, "We're coming," we stood, showed our boots, and for maybe forty yards we struggled downhill, complaining the whole time. Then, as Curly pulled ahead, I stepped on a sharp rock, lurched sideways, and come down with both feet on Curly's gun. That snatched Curly's foot out from under him. He yelled and went down. It weren't exactly how he planned it, but it surely made his fall look real.

Surprised us all, but I done some fast thinking right then. "He's snake bit!" I yelled. "Come help! I'll beat it with this here stick!" Heart in my throat, I knelt to pick up his carbine.

As I stood and cocked it, Squeak moved towards us and away from Miz Sentell, just as English Bob started uphill. The saddle tramp was froze, holding the arm of the minister's daughter. Lord Jim froze at first, then moved towards Miz Sentell.

I shot English Bob, and that fat slug knocked him flat. I know it was selfish, but he was closest to my boy Wade. I can tell you, that Big Fifty killed at both ends. Like to broke my shoulder.

Squeak snapped off a shot at us and yelled, "You damn—" something or other, then swung to cover Miz Sentell. Lord Jim stepped in front of her as Squeak fired. Squeak shrieked like a woman, "You traitor!"

His shot punched them both over the ledge. A Colt .45 will do that.

Curly untied that bullwhip, quick as you please, then sat up and shot Squeak. That little .38 staggered Squeak, who fired another shot at us, then took a step toward the ledge and started to point his revolver over the ledge. Curly's second shot knocked Squeak sideways, and I finally got Curly's lever unlocked and jacked in another round. My second shot flipped Squeak over the side.

The saddle tramp said, "Don't shoot or I'll kill her." He pointed his pistol at us and his finger at the minister's daughter. Big mistake. Wade picked up the Englishman's pistol and fired, hitting the tramp in the thigh. His gun went off as he started to fall sideways.

I shot him, too. My shot hit him in the chest, and he went flat on his back. Somewhere in the middle of this somebody shot me in the leg. I never figured whether it was Squeak or the tramp.

Suddenly there weren't nobody standing on the ledge but Wade and the girl. He kept swinging that revolver between the two downed men, but it turned out their hash had been cooked. The girl moved up against Wade's back.

Me and Curly stumbled down to the ledge, both of us cussing the hard rocks and sandburs, then us and Wade leaned over the edge. The others was on another small ledge, maybe ten feet down. Lord Jim was half laying on Miz Sentell, moaning and groaning. There was blood on both of them.

"I'm beat up some, but I'm all right," she said. "Jim saved me. Help him. His leg is mangled, and he's shot. He took the bullet." She squirmed to ease out from under him.

Squeak was in a jumble, several yards off to their left. One leg was at a funny angle, clearly broke, and he was covered in blood. But he was alive.

"I'm shot to rags," he squeaked. "Help me."

Curly said, "Untie that bullwhip from my carbine."

I unsnaggled the whip from his gun's lever and held it out to him. I was took aback.

"You gonna whip him now? Right now, with me and Jim needing bandaging?"

He stared at me for a second. "You really do think I'm crazy, don't you? Just hand me my carbine and go help my wife. And quit whining."

He snatched the gun from me, leaned over the ledge, and shot Squeak four more times. Each shot from that Big Fifty bounced Squeak's scrawny body right off the ground. He finally slid off that ledge and on down the hill in a small rockslide.

By then, me and Wade was halfway down to Miz Sentell and Lord Jim. Wade said, "I'd say Squeak is done, Marshal."

"That'll do," he said. "And I ain't no marshal."

Back to normal. Finally.

We was all on the wagon on the way home, except for Wade. Wade had rode on ahead to let folks at the ranch know what happened. Curly drove, and Miz Sentell sat up front, too, hugging the preacher's daughter in betwixt them. Me and Lord Jim was doctored up with bandages and laudanum, laying on our bedrolls in the back.

In a low voice, I said, "Tell me true, Jim. Was you working them on the inside all along? Not that it matters now."

He gave me a dopey smile. "Or did I just have a late fit of conscience and change sides right at the end. That is what you are asking, isn't it?"

I mumbled, "You know what I'm asking."

"Conscience is not my strong suit," he said. "My father ran off or died before I knew him. My sergeant might have filled that void, but he liked to, ah, take advantage of young soldiers. I deserted and jumped a ship to here. After I stabbed him."

"So?"

"So I never had a real father. Curly Jack Sentell is the closest I've come. I could never go against him. I just thought I had best keep Squeak close, especially after he told me what he planned to do here. He trusted me. Kept saying how intelligent I was, despite my lack of education. I truly believe my English accent had him fooled, since he kept running into me and confiding in me. You know he meant to murder you, Wade, and Curly right here, then ride to the ranch, rob it, and abduct Emmalee also? Did you know?"

All I could say was, "Judas Priest!"

Lord Jim said, "I thought maybe I could swing the balance, since I could not see how you would defeat his plan and had no way to warn you."

Over his shoulder, Curly growled, "I heard that. I ain't about to take on no stepson at my age."

It was almost quiet then, as we thumped and bumped and jangled east into the darkness. The rain had quit, and the sun was setting behind us over the lake, all gold and pink and blue.

The girl looked sideways at Curly and said, "I hope you ain't gonna hang Mister Jim. He weren't part of that attack on my family." She paused. "And after he come into the gang, he tried to keep them others off me."

Miz Sentell leaned over and punched Curly's shoulder.

He grunted and said, "I might could hire a crippled cook, could he fix beans better'n that durn Mex I got now. All you foreigners is good cooks, I hear."

We might have rode another half a mile when Curly looked over at the young girl. "I know what happened to your family, child, and I'm sorry." He shook his head. "Ain't nobody knows what you been through."

She nodded.

"We found some cash on them, which we'll get back to the folks in your parish. Now, I would like to know your name."

"Sarah," she said in a low voice. "But my Daddy always called me Calico." She sobbed suddenly, then moaned, "He's gone now. They're all gone."

Miz Sentell hugged her tight, then said, "I always wanted a daughter. Now, now. You go right ahead and cry this all out. We'll be home soon."

Curly looked back at me and rolled his eyes. "Oh, hell," he said. "Here we go."

Miz Sentell said, "You watch your mouth, and I need to ask you something, John Sentell. Did you even bring the ransom money?"

He shrugged and said, "Wasn't no need, was there? Things turned out all right."

"I cannot believe you!" she snapped. "I never-ever in my life have I even *heard* of such a thing! The supreme arrogance of it!" She turned and glared at me. "Were you aware?"

He saved me from answering. In his best soothing voice, he said, "Now, now, Missus. Go easy. I was just yanking your chain. It's right here in my money pouch." He patted his belly. Lord Jim was snoring a soft purr, kind of like Emmalee. I slid off to sleep. I might have been smiling.

ABOUT THE AUTHOR

McKendree R. (Mike) Long III is a retired soldier with two combat tours in Viet Nam. His awards include the Silver Star, Parachutist Badge, and the Combat Infantryman's Badge. He and his wife, Mary, have two married daughters, four grandchildren, and five great-grands. He holds a B.S. in business administration and is also a retired financial consultant. He is a member of Western Writers of America, South Carolina Writers Association, Military Writers Society of America, and Western Fictioneers.

The employees of Five Star Publishing hope you have enjoyed this book.

Our Five Star novels explore little-known chapters from America's history, stories told from unique perspectives that will entertain a broad range of readers.

Other Five Star books are available at your local library, bookstore, all major book distributors, and directly from Five Star/Gale.

Connect with Five Star Publishing

Visit us on Facebook:
https://www.facebook.com/FiveStarCengage

Email:
FiveStar@cengage.com

For information about titles and placing orders:
(800) 223-1244
gale.orders@cengage.com

To share your comments, write to us:
Five Star Publishing
Attn: Publisher
10 Water St., Suite 310
Waterville, ME 04901